Also by Lucia Berlin

A Manual for Cleaning Ladies (1977)

Angels Laundromat (1981)

Legacy (1983)

Phantom Pain (1984)

Safe & Sound (1988)

Homesick: New & Selected Stories (1990)

Where I Live Now: Stories 1993–1998 (1999)

A Manual for Cleaning Women: Selected Stories (2015)

Lucia Berlin

SO LONG

Stories: 1987–1992

Black Sparrow Books

David R. Godine, Publisher

BOSTON

This is
A Black Sparrow Book
Published in 2016 by
DAVID R. GODINE, PUBLISHER
Post Office Box 450
Jaffrey, New Hampshire 03452
www.blacksparrowbooks.com

Copyright © 1993 by Lucia Berlin
Copyright © 2016 by the Literary Estate of Lucia Berlin LP

All rights reserved. No part of this book may be used or reproduced without written permission from the publisher, except in the case of brief quotations embodied in critical articles and reviews. For information, contact Permissions, David R. Godine, Publisher, Fifteen Court Square, Suite 320, Boston, Massachusetts, 02108.

ACKNOWLEDGMENTS

Some of these stories first appeared in *Phantom Pain*, Tombouctou Press (1984) and *Safe and Sound*, Poltroon Press (1989). Some of the stories also appeared in the following magazines: *City Lights Review, Folio, Gas, In This Corner, Jejune, Peninsula, Rigorous, Rolling Stock, The New Censorship* and *Zyzzyva*. Many thanks to those publishers for permission to reprint.

Black Sparrow Press books are printed on acid-free paper.

LIBRARY OF CONGRESS CATALOGING-IN-PUBLICATION DATA
Berlin, Lucia.
So long : stories, 1987–1992 / Lucia Berlin.
p.   cm.
ISBN 0-87685-894-9 (cloth) : $25.00.
ISBN 0-87685-893-0 (pbk.) : $13.00.
ISBN 0-87685-895-7 (cloth signed) : $30.00
I. Title.
PS 3552.E72485S6   1993
813'.54–dc20   93-6659
CIP

Second printing, 2016
Printed in the United States

For Monica

Contents

Luna Nueva

The sun set with a hiss as the wave hit the beach. The woman continued up the checkered black and gold tiles of the *malecón* to the cliffs on the hill. Other people resumed walking too once the sun had set, like spectators leaving a play. It isn't just the beauty of the tropical sunset she thought, the importance of it. In Oakland the sun set into the Pacific each evening and it was the end of another day. When you travel you step back from your own days, from the fragmented imperfect linearity of your time. As when reading a novel, the events and people become allegorical and eternal. The boy whistles on a wall in Mexico. Tess leans her head against a cow. They will keep doing that forever; the sun will just keep on falling into the sea.

She walked onto a platform above the cliffs. The magenta sky reflected iridescent in the water. Below the cliffs a vast swimming pool had been built of stones into the jagged rock. Waves shattered against the far walls and spilled into the pool, scattering crabs. A few boys swam in the deeper water, but most people waded or sat on the mossy rocks.

The woman climbed down the rocks to the water. She took off the shift covering her bathing suit and sat on the slippery wall with the others. They watched as the sky faded and a new orange moon appeared in the mauve sky. *La luna!* people cried. *Luna nueva!* The evening grew dark and the orange moon turned to gold. The foam cascading into the pool was a sharp metallic white: the clothes of the bathers flowed eerie white as if under a strobe light.

Most of the bathers in the silver pool were fully clothed. Many of them had come from the mountains or ranchos far away; their baskets lay in piles on the rocks.

And they couldn't swim, so it was nice to lie suspended in the pool, for the waves to rock them and swirl them back and forth. When the breakers covered the wall it didn't seem that they were in a pool at all, but in their own calm eddy in the middle of the ocean.

Street lights came on above them against the palms on the *malecón*. The lights glowed like amber lanterns on their intricate wrought-iron poles. The water in the pool reflected the lights over and over, first whole, then into dazzling fragments, then whole again like full moons under the tiny moon in the sky.

The woman dove into the water. The air was cool, the water warm and salty. Crabs raced over her feet, the stones underfoot were velvety and jagged. She remembered only then being in that pool many years ago, before her children could swim. A sharp memory of her husband's eyes looking at her across the pool. He held one of their sons as she swam with the other in her arms. No pain accompanied the sweetness of this recollection. No loss or regret or foretaste of death. Gabriel's eyes. Her sons' laughter, echoing from the cliffs into the water.

The bathers' voices ricocheted too from the stone. Ah! they cried, as at fireworks, when the young boys dove into the water. They swayed in their white clothes. It was festive, with the clothes swirling, as if they were waltzing at a ball. Beneath them, the sea made delicate traceries on the sand. A young couple knelt in the water. They didn't touch, but were so in love it seemed to the woman that tiny darts and arrows shot out into the water from them, like fireflies or phosphorescent fish. They wore white clothes, but seemed naked against the dark sky. Their clothes clung to their black bodies, to his strong shoulders and loins, her breasts and belly. When the waves flowed in and ebbed out, her long hair floated up and covered them in tendrils of black fog and then subsided black and inky into the water.

A man wearing a straw hat asked the woman if she would take his babies out into the water. He handed her the smallest one, who was frightened. It slipped up through the woman's arms like a skittish baboon and climbed onto her head, tearing at her hair, coiling its legs and tail around her neck. She untangled herself from the screaming baby. Take the other one, the tame one, the man said, and that child did lie placidly while she swam with it in the water. So quiet she thought it must be asleep, but no it was humming. Other people sang and hummed in the cool night. The sliver of moon turned white like the foam as more people came down the stairs into the water. After a while the man took the baby from her and left then, with his children.

On the rocks a girl tried to coax her grandmother into the pool. No! No! I'll fall! Come in, the woman said, I'll take you swimming all around the pool.

"You see I broke my leg and I'm afraid I'll break it again."

"When did it happen?" the woman asked.

"Ten years ago. It was a terrible time. I couldn't chop firewood. I couldn't work in the fields. We had no food."

"Come in. I'll be careful of your leg."

At last the old lady let her lift her down from the rock and into the water. She laughed, clasping her frail arms around the woman's neck. She was light, like a bag of shells. Her hair smelled of charcoal fires. *Qué maravilla!* she whispered into the woman's throat. Her silver braid wafted out behind them in the water.

She was seventy-eight and had never seen the ocean before. She lived on a rancho near Chalchihuitles. She had ridden on the back of a truck to the seaport with her granddaughter.

"My husband died last month."

"*Lo siento.*"

She swam with the old lady to the far wall where the cool waves spilled over them.

"God finally took him, finally answered my prayers. Eight years he lay in bed. Eight years he couldn't talk, couldn't get up or feed himself. Lay like a baby. I would ache from being tired, my eyes would burn. At last, when I thought he was asleep I would try to steal away. He would whisper my name, a horrid croaking sound. *Consuelo! Consuelo!* and his skeleton hands, dead lizard hands would claw out to me. It was a terrible, terrible time."

"*Lo siento,*" the woman said again.

"Eight years. I could go nowhere. Not even to the corner. *Ni hasta la esquina!* Every night I prayed to the Virgin to take him, to give me some time, some days without him."

The woman clasped the old lady and swam out again into the pool, holding the frail body close to her.

"My mother died only six months ago. It was the same for me. A terrible, terrible time. I was tied to her day and night. She didn't know me and said ugly things to me, year after year, clawing at me."

Why am I telling this old lady such a lie? she wondered. But it wasn't such a lie, the bloody grasp.

"They're gone now," Consuelo said. "We are liberated."

The woman laughed; liberated was such an American word. The old lady thought she laughed because she was happy. She hugged the woman tightly and kissed her cheek. She had no teeth so the kiss was soft as mangos.

"The Virgin answered my prayers!" she said. "It pleases God, to see that you and I are free."

Back and forth the two women flowed in the dark water, the clothes of the bathers swirling around them like a ballet. Near them the young couple kissed, and for a moment there was a sprinkle of stars overhead, then a mist covered them and the moon and dimmed the opal lamplight from the street.

Luna Nueva

"Vamos a comer, abuelita!" the granddaughter called. She shivered, her dress dripping on the stones. A man lifted the old woman from the water, carried her up the winding rocks to the *malecón.* Mariachis played, far away.

"Adiós!" The old woman waved from the parapet.

"Adiós!"

The woman waved back. She floated at the far edge in the silken warm water. The breeze was inexpressibly gentle.

Sombra

The waiter retrieved her napkin from the floor, slid it onto her lap, his other hand swirled a plate of pastel fruit onto the table before her. Music came from everywhere, not transistors walking down city streets, but far away mariachis, a *bolero* on a radio in the kitchen, the whistle of the knife sharpener, an organ grinder, workmen singing from a scaffold.

Jane was a retired teacher, divorced, her children grown. She hadn't been in Mexico for twenty years, not since she had lived there with Sebastian and their sons, in Oaxaca.

She had always liked traveling alone. But yesterday, at Teotihuacan, it was so magnificent she had wanted to say it out loud, to confirm the color of the *maguey*.

She had liked being alone in France, being able to wander anywhere, talk to people. Mexico was hard. The warmth of the Mexicans accentuated her loneliness, the lost past.

This morning she had stopped at the Majestic desk and joined a guided group to the Sunday bullfights. The immense plaza, the fans, were daunting to face alone. *Fanático*, Spanish for fan. Imagine 50,000 Mexicans arriving on time, long before four o'clock, when the gates were locked. Out of respect for the bulls, her cab driver said.

The bullfight group assembled in the lobby at two-thirty. There were two American couples. The Jordans and the McIntyres. The men were surgeons, at a convention in Mexico City.

They were tennis-fit and tanned. Their wives were expensively dressed, but in that time warp doctors' wives have, wearing pant-suits fashionable back when they put their husbands through medical school. The women wore cheap black felt Spanish hats, with a red rose, that were sold on the streets as souvenirs. They thought they were "fun hats," not realizing how coquettish and pretty they looked in them.

There were four Japanese tourists. The Yamatos, an old couple in black traditional clothes. Their son, Jerry, a tall, handsome man in his forties, with a young Japanese bride, Deedee, dressed in American jeans and a sweatshirt. She and Jerry spoke English to each other, Japanese to his parents. She blushed when he kissed her neck or caught her fingers between his teeth.

It turned out that Jerry too was a Californian, an architect, Deedee a chemistry student in San Francisco. They would be in Mexico City for two more days. His parents had come from Tokyo to join them. No, they had never seen a bullfight, but Jerry thought it would seem very Japanese, combining what Mishima called Japanese qualities of elegance and brutality.

Jane was pleased that he should say something like that to her, almost a stranger, liked him immediately.

The three spoke about Mishima, and Mexico, as they all sat on leather sofas, waiting for the guide. Jane told the couple that she had spent her own honeymoon in Mexico City, too.

"It was wonderful," she said. "Magic. You could see the volcanoes then." Why do I keep thinking about Sebastian, anyway? I'll call him tonight, and tell him I went to the Plaza Mexico.

Señor Errazuriz looked like an old bullfighter himself, lean, regal. His too-long greasy hair curled in a perhaps unintentional *colita*. He introduced himself, asked them to relax, have a sangria while he told them a little about the *corridas*, gave a concise history and an explanation of what they were to expect. "The form of each *corrida* as timeless and precise as a musical score. But with each bull, the element of surprise."

Sombra

He told them to take something warm, even though now it was a hot day. Obediently they all went for sweaters, got into an already crowded elevator. *Buenas tardes.* It is a custom in Mexico to greet people you join in an elevator, in line at the post office, in a waiting room. It makes waiting easier, actually, and in an elevator you don't have to stare straight ahead because now you have acknowledged one another.

They all got into a hotel van. The two women continued a conversation about a manic depressive called Sabrina, begun back in Petaluma or Sausalito. The American doctors seemed ill at ease. The older Yamatos spoke softly in Japanese, looked down at their laps. Jerry and Deedee looked at each other, or smiled for photographs they had Jane take of them, in the hotel, in the van, in front of the fountain. The two doctors braked and cringed as the van sped down Insurgentes toward the plaza.

Jane sat in the front with Señor Errazuriz. They spoke in Spanish. He told her they were lucky to see Jorge Gutierrez today, the best matador in Mexico. There would also be a fine Spaniard, Roberto Dominguez, and a young Mexican making his debut, his *alternativa*, in the plaza, Alberto Giglio. Those aren't very romantic names, Jane commented, Gutierrez and Dominguez.

"They haven't earned an *apodo* like 'El Litri,'" he said.

Jerry caught Jane looking at him and his wife as they kissed. He smiled at her.

"Forgive me, I didn't mean to be rude," she said, but she was blushing too, like the girl.

"You must be thinking of your own honeymoon!" he grinned.

They parked the van near the stadium and a boy with a rag began washing the windows. Years ago there were parking meters in Mexico, but nobody collected the money or enforced the tickets. People used slugs or simply smashed the meters, as they did with the pay phones. So now the pay phones are free and there are no parking meters. But it seems as if each parking spot has its own private valet, who will watch your car, a boy appearing from nowhere.

Electric, exhilarating, the excitement of the crowd outside the plaza. "Feels like the World Series!" said one of the doctors. Stands sold tacos, posters, bulls' horns, capes, photographs of Dominguín, Juan Belmonte, Manolete. A huge bronze statue of El Armillita stood outside the arena. Some fans laid carnations at his feet. They had to bend down to do this, so it seemed as if they were genuflecting before him.

The groups' bags were searched by heavily armed security guards. All women, as were most of the guards all over Mexico. The entire Cuernavaca police force is female, Señor Errazuriz told Jane. Narcs, motorcycle cops, chief of police. Women are not so susceptible to bribery and corruption. Jerry said he had noticed how many women there were in public office, more than in the U.S.

"Of course. Our whole country is protected by the Virgin of Guadalupe!"

"Not that many female bullfighters, though?"

"A few. Good ones. But, really, it is for men to fight against the bulls."

Below in the plaza *monosabios* in red and white uniforms raked the sand. Pointillist whirls of color as the spectators climbed far up in the tiers to the blue circle of sky. Vendors carrying heavy buckets of beer and coke scampered along the metal rims above the cement seats, ran up and down stairs as narrow as on the pyramid of Teotihuacan. The group looked at their programs, the photographs and statistics of the toreros, of the bulls from the Santiago herd.

Men in black leather suits, smoking cigars, *charros* in big hats and silver decorated coats gathered around the *barrera*. Except for the two Spanish hats, their group was definitely underdressed. They had all come as for a ball game. Most of

Sombra

the Mexican and Spanish women were dressed casually, but as elegantly as possible, with heavy makeup and jewelry.

Their seats were in the shade. The plaza was perfectly divided into *sol y sombra*. The sun was bright.

At five minutes to four six *monosabios* walked around the plaza bearing aloft a cloth banner painted with the message, "If anyone is surprised throwing cushions they will be fined."

At four o'clock the trumpets played the opening thrilling *paso doble*. "Carmen!" Mrs. Jordan cried. The gate opened and the procession began. First the *alguaciles*, two black-bearded men on Arabian horses, dressed in black, starched white ruffs, plumed hats. Their fine horses pranced and strutted and reared as they crossed the plaza. Just behind them were the three matadors in glittering suits of light, embroidered capes over their left shoulders. Dominguez in black, Gutierrez in turquoise and Giglio in white. Behind each matador followed his *cuadrilla* of three men, also carrying elaborate capes. Then the fat picadors on padded, blind-folded horses, then the *monosabios* and *areneros*, in red and white. The men who actually removed the dead bulls were dressed in blue. In the last century in Madrid there was a popular group of trained monkeys performing in a theatre, whose costumes were the same as the men who worked in the bull-rings. They were called the Wise Monkeys—*monosabios*. The name stuck for the men in the *corridas*.

The toreros all wore salmon-colored stockings, ballet slippers which seemed incongruously flimsy. No, they have to feel the sand. Their feet are the most important part, Señor Errazuriz said. He noticed how Jane liked the colors and the clothes, the quilted, tufted upholsteries covering the picadors' horses. He told her that in Spain the matadors were starting to wear white stockings, but most true aficionados were against this.

A *monosabio* came out of the *torillo* gate and held up a wooden sign painted with "Chirusín 499 kilos." The trumpet sounded and the bull burst into the ring.

So Long: Stories

The first *tercio* was beautiful. Giglio made graceful swirling *faenas*. His *traje de luces* sparkled and shimmered in the late sun, turning into an aura of light around him. Except for a rhythmic *olé* during the passes, the plaza was silent. You could hear Chirusín's hooves, his breath, the rustle of the pink cape. *"Torero!"* the crowd yelled, and the young bullfighter smiled, a guileless smile of pure joy. This was his debut and he was welcomed wildly by the fans. There were many whistles though, too, because the bull wasn't brave, Señor Errazuriz said. The trumpet sounded for the entrance of the picadors, and the *peones* danced the bull to the horse. It was undeniably lovely.

The Americans were lulled by the ballet-like grace of the bullfight, surprised and sickened when the picador began jabbing the long hook into the back of the bull's *morrillo*, again and again. Blood spurted thick and glistening red. The fans whistled, the entire arena was whistling. They always do, Señor Errazuriz said, but he doesn't stop until the matador says so. Giglio nodded and the trumpets played, signalling the next *tercio*. Giglio placed the three pairs of white *banderillas* himself, running lightly toward Chirusín, dancing, whirling in the center of the ring, just missing the horns as he stabbed them perfectly, symmetrically each time until there were six white banners above the flowing red blood. The Yamatos smiled.

Giglio was so graceful, so happy that everyone who watched felt delight. Still, it's a bad bull, dangerous, Señor Errazuriz said. The crowd gave the young man all their encouragement, he had such *trapío*, style. But he could not kill the bull. Once, twice, then again and again. Chirusín hemorrhaged from his mouth but would not fall. The *banderilleros* ran the bull in circles to hasten its death as Giglio plunged the sword still once more.

"Barbaric," Dr. McIntyre said. The two American surgeons rose as one, and took their wives away with them. The women in their pretty hats kept pausing on the steep stairway to look back. Señor Errazuriz said he would see them to a cab, and pay it of course. He would be right back.

The old Yamatos politely watched Chirusín die. The young couple was thrilled. The *corrida* was powerful, majestic to them. At last the bull lay down and died and Giglio withdrew the bloody sword. Mules dragged away the bull, to whistles and jeers from the crowd. They blamed the bad kill on the bull, not on the young matador. Jorge Gutierrez, his *padrino*, embraced Giglio.

There was a frenzy of activity before the next *corrida*. People ran up and down visiting, smoking, drinking beer, squirting wine into their mouths. Vendors sold *alegrías* and bright green oval pastries, pistachio nuts, pig skins, Domino pizzas.

There was a warm breeze and Jane shuddered. A wave of the deepest fear came over her, a sense of impermanence. The entire plaza might disappear.

"You are cold," Jerry said. "Here, put on your sweater."

"Thanks," she said.

Deedee reached across Jerry's lap and touched Jane's arm.

"We'll take you outside, if you want to leave."

"No, thank you. I think it must be the altitude."

"It gets to Jerry, too. He has a pacemaker; sometimes it's hard to breathe."

"You're still trembling," Jerry said. "Sure you're ok?"

The couple smiled at her with kindness. She smiled back, but was still shaken by an awareness of our insignificance. Nobody even knew where she was.

"Oh, good, you're in time," she said when Señor Errazuriz returned.

"I don't understand it," he said. "I, myself, I can't watch American films. *Goodfellas, Miami Blues.* That is cruelty to me." He shrugged. To the Yamatos he apologized for the bulls from Santiago, as if they were a national embarrassment. The Japanese man was equally polite in his reassurances that on the contrary, they were grateful to be here. Bullfighting was a fine art, exquisite. It is a rite, Jane thought as the trumpet sounded. Not a performance, a sacrament to death.

The coliseum pulsated, throbbed with cries of Jorge, Jorge. Whistles and angry jeers at the judge. *Culero!* Asshole! because he didn't get rid of the bull, Platero. *No se presta,* he doesn't lend himself, Señor Errazuriz said. In the second *tercio* the bull stumbled and fell, and then just sat there, as if he just didn't feel like getting up. *"La Golondrina! La Golondrina!"* a group in the sunny section chanted.

Señor Errazuriz said that was a song about swallows leaving, a farewell song. "They're saying, 'Goodbye with this *pinche* bull!'" Jorge was obviously disgusted, and decided to kill Platero as soon as possible. But he couldn't. Like Giglio before him he bounced the sword off the bull, jabbed it too high, too far back. Finally the animal died. The bullfighter left the ring downcast, humiliated. The continued chants of *"torero"* from his loyal fans must have felt like mockery. The *monosabios* and mules came for Platero, who was dragged away to whistles and curses, thousands of flying cushions.

Whereas Giglio had been lyrical and Gutierrez formal, authoritative, the young Spaniard, Dominguez, was fiery and defiant, sweeping the bull Centenario after him across the sand, flaring his cape like a peacock. He stood with pelvis arched inches from the bull. *Olé, olé.* The matador and bull swirled like water plants. The picadors entered the ring, the *banderilleros* took turns. Capes swaying, they lured the bull toward the horse. The bull attacked the belly of the horse. Again and again the picador thrust the spear into the bull. Furious, then, the bull pawed the sand, his head lowered, then thundered toward the nearest *banderillero.*

At that moment a man leaped into the field. He was young, dressed in jeans and a white shirt, carrying a red shawl. He raced past the subalterns, faced the bull, and executed a lovely pass. *Olé.* The entire plaza was in an uproar, cheering and whistling, throwing hats. *"Un Espontáneo!"* Two policemen in grey flannel suits jumped into the arena and chased after the man, running clumsily in the sand in their high-heeled boots. Dominguez gracefully fought the bull whenever it came his way. Centenario thought it was a party, jumped up and down like a playful labrador, charged first a *subalterno*, then a guard, then a horse, then the man's red shawl. Wham—he tried to knock over a picador, then raced to get the two policemen, knocking them both down, wounding one, crushing his foot. All three subalterns were chasing the man, but stopped and waited each time the man fought the bull.

"El Espontáneo! El Espontáneo!" cried the crowd, but more police entered and tossed him over the *barrera* to waiting handcuffs. He was taken into custody. There was a stiff sentence and fine for "spontaneous ones," Señor Errazuriz said, otherwise people would do it all the time. But the crowds kept cheering for him as the wounded guard was carried away and the picadors left, to the music.

Dominguez was going to dedicate the bull. He asked the judge permission to dedicate it to the *espontáneo*, and for him to be set free. It was granted. The man was taken out of handcuffs. He leapt the *barrera* again, this time to accept the bullfighter's *montera*, and to embrace him. Hats and jackets sailed from the stands to his feet. He bowed, with the grace of a torero, jumped the fence and climbed way, way up into the sunny stands, up by the clock. Meanwhile the *banderilleros* were distracting the bull, who was totally ruined now, like a hyperactive child, careening around the ring, ramming his horns into the wooden fence and the *burladeros* where the *cuadrilla* hid. Still everyone merrily sang *"El Espontáneo!"* Even the old Japanese were shouting it! The young couple were laughing, hugging each other. What a glorious, dazzling confusion.

Dominguez was denied a change of bull, but managed to fight the nervous animal with spirit and much daring, since

So Long: Stories

Centenario had become erratic and angry. Whenever he tried to kill the bull, it shied and jumped. Catch me if you can! So again there were repeated bloody stabbings in the wrong places.

Jane thought that Jerry was yelling at the matador, but he had simply cried out, tried to stand. He fell onto the cement stairs. His head had cracked against the cement, was bleeding red into his black hair. Deedee knelt on the stairs next to him.

"It's too soon," she said.

Jane sent a guard for a doctor. Jerry's parents knelt side by side on the step above him while vendors scurried up and down past them. With a hysterical giggle Jane noticed that whereas in the States a crowd would have gathered, no one in the plaza took their eyes from the ring, where Giglio fought a new bull, Navegante.

The doctor arrived as just below them the picador was stabbing the bull, to fierce whistles and protests. Sweating, the little man waited until the noise abated, abstractedly holding Jerry's hand. When the picadors left he said to Deedee, "He is dead." But she knew that, his parents knew. The old man held his wife as they looked down on him. They looked at their son with sorrow. Deedee had turned him over. His face had an amused expression, his eyes were half-open. Deedee smiled down at him. A raincoat vendor covered him with blue plastic. "Thank you," Deedee said. "Five thousand pesos, please."

Olé, olé. Giglio whirled in the ring, the *banderillas* poised above his head. With an undulating zig-zag he danced toward the bull. Two women guards came. They couldn't get a gurney down the steps, one of them told Jane. They would have to wait until the *corrida* was over to bring one to the *callejón*, then his body could be lifted over the *barrera*. No problem. They would come as soon as they could get through. Another guard told Jerry's parents they had to return to their sets, they might be hurt. Obediently the elderly couple sat down. They waited, whispering. Señor Errazuriz spoke to them gently and

Sombra

they nodded, although they didn't understand. Deedee held her husband's head in her lap. She gripped Jane's hand, stared unseeing into the ring where Giglio was exchanging swords for the kill. Jane spoke with the ambulance driver, translated for Deedee, took the American Express card from Jerry's wallet.

"Has he been very ill?" Jane asked Deedee.

"Yes," she whispered. "But we thought there was more time."

Jane and Deedee embraced, the arm-rest between them pressing into their bodies like sadness.

"Too soon," Deedee said again.

The plaza was on its feet. Jorge had given Giglio an extra bull, Genovés, as a present for his *alternativa*. Before the next *corrida, areneros* in blue, with wheelbarrows, came to cover up the blood in the sand, others raked it smooth. The plaza was empty when the gurney wheeled up below the *barrera*. Meet us in front, the medics said, but Deedee refused to leave him. It took a long time to move Jerry's body, and to get him down through the now frenzied crowd and onto the gurney. Once in the *callejón* outside of the ring they kept having to wait, move out of the way of running *banderilleros*, of the man with water bottles to wet the red cape, the *mozo de las espadas*, the man who carried the swords. Indignant shouts at Deedee, because she was a woman, a taboo in the *callejón*.

Señor Errazuriz and Jane accompanied the old couple on the far, far climb to the top of the plaza. Giglio had killed Genovés with one perfect thrust. He was awarded two ears and a tail. The brave bull was being dragged triumphantly around the place to cries of *"Toro! Toro!"* People spilled onto the narrow steps, many drunk, all ecstatic. The *alquacil* was walking across the sand to Giglio, carrying the ears and the tail.

Jane walked behind the Yamatos. Señor Errazuriz and a guard led the way to the blare of trumpets, deafening shouts of *"Torero, torero."* Roses and carnations and hats flew through the air, darkening the sky.

Friends

Loretta met Anna and Sam the day she saved Sam's life.

Anna and Sam were old. She was 80 and he was 89. Loretta would see Anna from time to time when she went to swim at her neighbor Elaine's pool. One day she stopped by as the two women were convincing the old guy to take a swim. He finally got in, was dog-paddling along with a big grin on his face when he had a seizure. The other two women were in the shallow end and didn't notice. Loretta jumped in, shoes and all, pulled him to the steps and up out of the pool. He didn't need resuscitation but he was disoriented and frightened. He had some medicine to take, for epilepsy, and they helped him dry off and dress. They all sat around for a while until they were sure he was fine and could walk to their house, just down the block. Anna and Sam kept thanking Loretta for saving his life, and insisted that she go to lunch at their house the next day.

It happened that she wasn't working for the next few days. She had taken three days off without pay because she had a lot of things that needed doing. Lunch with them would mean going all the way back to Berkeley from the city, and not finishing everything in one day, as she had planned.

She often felt helpless in situations like this. The kind where you say to yourself, Gosh, it's the least I can do, they are so nice. If you don't do it you feel guilty and if you do you feel like a wimp.

So Long: Stories

She stopped being in a bad mood the minute she was inside their apartment. It was sunny and open, like an old house in Mexico, where they had lived most of their lives. Anna had been an archaeologist and Sam an engineer. They had worked together every day at Teotihuacan and other sites. Their apartment was filled with fine pottery and photographs, a wonderful library. Downstairs, in the back yard was a large vegetable garden, many fruit trees, berries. Loretta was amazed that the two bird-like, frail people did all the work themselves. Both of them used canes, and walked with much difficulty.

Lunch was toasted cheese sandwiches, chayote soup and a salad from their garden. Anna and Sam prepared the lunch together, set the table and served the lunch together.

They had done everything together for fifty years. Like twins, they each echoed the other or finished sentences the other had started. Lunch passed pleasantly as they told her, in stereo, some of their experiences working on the pyramid in Mexico, and about other excavations they had worked on. Loretta was impressed by these two old people, by their shared love of music and gardening, by their enjoyment of one another. She was amazed at how involved they were in local and national politics, going to marches and protests, writing congressmen and editors, making phone calls. They read three or four papers every day, read novels or history to each other at night.

While Sam was clearing the table with shaking hands, Loretta said to Anna how enviable it was to have such a close lifetime companion. Yes, Anna said, but soon one of us will be gone....

Loretta was to remember that statement much later, and wonder if Anna had begun to cultivate a friendship with her as a sort of insurance policy against the time when one of them would die. But, no, she thought, it was simpler than that. The two of them had been so self-sufficient, so enough for each other all their lives, but now Sam was becoming dreamy and often incoherent. He repeated the same stories over and over, and although Anna was always patient with him, Loretta felt that she was glad to have someone else to talk to.

Whatever the reason, she found herself more and more involved in Sam and Anna's life. They didn't drive anymore. Often Anna would call Loretta at work and ask her to pick up peat moss when she got off, or take Sam to the eye doctor. Sometimes both of them felt too bad to go to the store, so Loretta would pick things up for them. She liked them both, admired them. Since they seemed so much to want company she found herself at dinner with them once a week, every two weeks at the most. A few times she asked them to her house for dinner, but there were so many steps to climb and the two arrived so exhausted that she stopped. So then she would take fish or chicken or a pasta dish to their house. They would make a salad, serve berries from the garden for dessert.

After dinner, over cups of mint or jamaica tea they would sit around the table while Sam told stories. About the time Anna got polio, at a dig deep in the jungle in the Yucatán, how they got her to a hospital, how kind people were. Many stories about the house they built in Xalapa. The mayor's wife, the time she broke her leg climbing out of a window to avoid a visitor. Sam's stories always began, "That reminds me of the time . . ."

Little by little Loretta learned the details of their life story. Their courtship on Mount Tam. Their romance in New York while they were communists. Living in sin. They had never married, still took satisfaction in this unconventionality. They had two children; both lived in distant cities. There were stories about the ranch near Big Sur, when the children were little. As a story was ending Loretta would say, "I hate to leave, but I have to get to work very early tomorrow." Often she would leave then. Usually though, Sam would say, "Just let me tell you what happened to the wind-up phonograph." Hours later, exhausted, she would drive home to her house in Oakland, saying to herself that she couldn't keep on doing this. Or that she would keep going, but set a definite time limit.

It was not that they were ever boring or uninteresting. On the contrary, the couple had lived a rich full life, were involved and perceptive. They were intensely interested in the world, in their own past. They had such a good time, adding to the other's remarks, arguing about dates or details, that Loretta didn't have the heart to interrupt them and leave. And it did make her feel good to go there, because the two people were so glad to see her. But sometimes she felt like not going over at all, when she was too tired or had something else to do. Finally she did say that she couldn't stay so late, that it was hard to get up the next morning. Come for Sunday brunch, Anna said.

When the weather was fair they ate on a table on their porch, surrounded by flowers and plants. Hundreds of birds came to the feeders right by them. As it grew colder they ate inside by a cast-iron stove. Sam tended it with logs he had split himself. They had waffles or Sam's special omelette, sometimes Loretta brought bagels and lox. Hours went by, the day went by as Sam told his stories, with Anna correcting them and adding comments. Sometimes, in the sun on the porch or by the heat of the fire, it was hard to stay awake.

Their house in Mexico had been made of concrete block, but the beams and counters and cupboards had been made of cedar wood. First the big room—the kitchen and living room—was built. They had planted trees, of course, even before they started building the house. Bananas and plums, jacarandas. The next year they added a bedroom, several years later another bedroom and a studio for Anna. The beds, the workbenches and tables were made of cedar. They got home to their little house after working in the field, in another state in Mexico. The house was always cool and smelt of cedar, like a big cedar chest.

Anna got pneumonia and had to go to the hospital. As sick as she was, all she could think of was Sam, how he would get

Friends

along without her. Loretta promised her she would go by before work, see that he took his medication and had breakfast, that she would cook him dinner after work, take him to the hospital to see her.

The terrible part was that Sam didn't talk. He would sit shivering on the side of the bed as Loretta helped him dress. Mechanically he took his pills and drank pineapple juice, carefully wiped his chin after he ate breakfast. In the evening when she arrived he would be standing on the porch waiting for her. He wanted to go see Anna first, and then have dinner. When they got to the hospital, Anna lay pale, her long white braids hanging down like a little girl's. She had an IV, a catheter, oxygen. She didn't speak, but smiled and held Sam's hand while he told her how he had done a load of wash, watered the tomatoes, mulched the beans, washed dishes, made lemonade. He talked on to her, breathless, told her every hour of his day. When they left Loretta had to hold him tight, he stumbled and wavered as he walked. In the car going home he cried, he was so worried. But Anna came home and was fine, except that there was so much to be done in the garden. The next Sunday, after brunch, Loretta helped weed the garden, cut back blackberry vines. Loretta was worried then, what if Anna got really sick? What was she in for with this friendship? The couple's dependence upon one another, their vulnerability saddened and moved her. Those thoughts passed through her head as she worked, but it was nice, the cool black dirt, the sun on her back. Sam, telling his stories as he weeded the adjacent row.

The next Sunday that Loretta went to their house she was late. She had been up early, there had been many things to do. She really wanted to stay home, but didn't have the heart to call and cancel.

The front door was not unlatched, as usual, so she went to the garden, to go up the back steps. She walked into the garden to look around, it was lush with tomatoes, squash, snow

31

peas. Drowsy bees. Anna and Sam were outside on the porch upstairs. Loretta was going to call to them but they were talking very intently.

"She's never been late before. Maybe she won't come."

"Oh, she'll come . . . these mornings mean so much to her."

"Poor thing. She is so lonely. She needs us. We're really her only family."

"She sure enjoys my stories. Dang. I can't think of a single one to tell her today."

"Something will come to you. . . ."

"Hello!" Loretta called. "Anybody home?"

Our Lighthouse

Hi! I was dreaming! But not a dream with pictures. I could smell my mother's Swedish cookies. Right here in this room. Right here.

We lived in a lighthouse, me and my seven brothers and sisters, on the Sainte Marie River. There's no place to put things, much less hide them, in a lighthouse, but my ma sure could hide cookies. I always found them though. Under a washtub. A loaf of banana bread in my pa's boot!

Winters were hard, miserable when we had to move to town. To a one-room shack with a wood stove, all of us sleeping on the floor. My father worked in the train yards, when he got work. He hated it. He wasn't a drinker, but he got mean in winter and beat all of us and my ma, just out of being worn out and cooped up, away from the river.

None of us could ever hardly wait for spring. Every day as soon as the thaws started we'd be down checking out the locks, waiting for the filthy ice to break up and the boats to go through.

Seems like we never actually saw the last ice melt. One day you'd wake up and you could smell it in the air. Spring.

That first day was always the best day of the year, better than Christmas. Packing up the dory and the rowboats. Pa would be puffing on his pipe and whistling at the same time, smacking us all on the head to hurry. Ma would just load and load the boats with gear she'd had ready for weeks, singing hymns in Swedish.

So Long: Stories

Our lighthouse stood right smack in the middle of the river. On a concrete slab over high craggy rocks. Waves crashed up over the iron door sometimes so we'd have to wait to get in. A ladder spiraled round and round, high, up to the tower where you could see the whole wide world.

Now the lighthouse wasn't that much bigger than the shack in town. But it was cool and windows looked out onto the water and the forests on the shore. Water and birds all around. When the logs came crashing past us you could smell the sweet sap of pine, cedar. It's the most beautiful spot in the entire U.S. of A. What am I saying? Not now, not after the iron and copper people and Union Carbide got through with it. More and more locks, and the rapids are gone. The birds too, I expect. Heck, even the lighthouse is gone. Boats run all year long.

We thought we were special. We were, in our lighthouse. Even things like going to the bathroom. No toilet or outhouse, just went right over the side. There was something nice about that, part of the river. That river was clean and clear, exact same color as a Coca-Cola bottle.

Ma and Pa worked all day. He'd be checking the five light-houses, sanding, painting, oiling gears. Ma would cook and clean away. Everybody worked, sanding, scraping barnacles, patching. Well, I didn't work that much, never was much for work. I'd high-tail off in a skiff to the woods where I'd lie all day in the grass, under some spruce or hemlock tree. Flowers everywhere. No, sorry, I can't remember any names of flowers. Can't remember a damn thing anymore. Wild clematis, moon-weed, bittersweet! Ma had made me an oil-cloth sack to keep my books in. Never took it off. Even slept in it. Every Hardy Boys and western I could get my hands on. Sure! Sure you can bring me some Zane Greys! The most beautiful title ever written was *Riders of the Purple Sage*.

Early evening us kids would set out in the row-boat to fire up the lamps in the smaller lighthouses, on Sugar Island, Neebish, and two other points. Ed and George and Will and me, we'd fight over who got to do it, every damn time. Ed was the oldest. He had a mean streak. He'd pull the plug in the boat and just laugh, holding it out far over the water. Rest of us would have to bail like crazy not to swamp.

He still has a mean streak. Married to a mean old woman too. Captain of one of Ford's river boats. George is Fire Chief of Sault Sainte Marie. Oh, you know. I mean they were. They're all dead now. Been dead for years. I'm all that's left. Ninety-five and can't walk, can't even hold up my head.

I wish I could say I'd been a better son. I was always a dreamer. A reader and a lover. In love every year, ever since kindergarten. Swear I was just as in love with Martha Sorensen when I was five years as I was when I got grown. And women, they all fell for me. I was a good-looker. No, don't you be kidding me, I'm just an old shell now. Steve McQueen? Yeah, that's my style... you got that right.

Lucille, my wife. We met in Detroit. It was love at first sight. *Never* was a love, a romance, like between us two. And it just kept on. She's starting to hate me now, I can tell. No, she isn't patient, either. I ask for orange juice and she hollers, "Wait a minute. Don't get your shorts in a knot!" I wish I'd die today, just die, before she stops loving me.

I was twelve when my father was killed. 1916. We were in town. Bitter, cruel winter. He was working as a brakeman for the B & O line in the middle of a blizzard. Snow and wind howling so loud he didn't see or hear the locomotive. Ran right over him. It was terrible, terrible. You must think me a baby, bawling like this. He was a big man. Fine man.

They took up a collection for us after the funeral. We were glad because there was nothing to eat. $50. You know they say, well, money went further in those days. $50. It was nothing, for eight of us. We all just wept.

Ed and George quit school and worked on the boats. Will

became a Western Union boy. My sisters did housework. I wouldn't quit school, but delivered papers mornings and nights. Dark and cold and snow bound. I hated it.

I admit it. I was bitter. Sorry for myself. Missed the lighthouse and just plain hated being so poor. Mostly it killed my pride to look shabby, to wear cheap shoes. Anyway when I was fifteen I ran away to Detroit. Got a dishwashing job and took up with an older woman. Gloria. A looker, with green eyes. Boy did I fall for her. She was a drinker, though. Whew, that's another story.

Soon as I could I became a bartender, and that's what I did all my life. Liked it, too. No, never was a drinking man. No excuse for being so ornery.

I only went back once. When my ma died. Thirty, forty years ago. Like to have broke my heart. They were all still mad at me, for running out on them and ma. And they were right. I had to swallow my pride and take their hatred. I deserved it. And I loved my ma. She and I were a lot alike. Daydreamers. I was ashamed I never once wrote her or went to see her before she died. Well, it was too late.

Got me a boat and went out to the lighthouse. Came pretty close to throwing myself off, I felt so rotten. Cried all day and night. Worst night of my life.

At night, from where we slept, as kids, we could watch the arc of the big light, intersecting with the signals from the other lighthouses. And in between there'd be stars, a million stars. All night long the boats would pass by. Whisper past like ghosts, rippling the water.

Unmanageable

In the deep dark night of the soul the liquor stores and bars are closed. She reached under the mattress; the pint bottle of vodka was empty. She got out of bed, stood up. She was shaking so badly that she sat down on the floor. She was hyperventilating. If she didn't get a drink she would go into d.t.'s or have a seizure.

Trick is to slow down your breathing and your pulse. Stay as calm as you can until you can get a bottle. Sugar. Tea with sugar, that's what they gave you in detox. But she was shaking too hard to stand. She lay on the floor breathing deep yoga breaths. Don't think, God don't think about the state you're in or you will die, of shame, a stroke. Her breath slowed down. She started to read titles of books in the bookcase. Concentrate, read them out loud. Edward Abbey, Chinua Achebe, Sherwood Anderson, Jane Austen, Paul Auster, don't skip, slow down. By the time she had read the whole wall of books she was better. She pulled herself up. Holding on to the wall, shaking so badly she could barely move each foot, she made it to the kitchen. No vanilla. Lemon extract. It seared her throat and she retched, held her mouth shut to reswallow it. She made some tea, thick with honey, sipped it slowly in the dark. At 6, in two hours, the Uptown liquor store in Oakland would sell her some vodka. In Berkeley you had to wait until 7. Oh, god, did she have any money? She crept back to her room to check in her purse on the desk. Her son Nick must have taken her wallet and car keys. She couldn't look for them in her sons' room without waking them.

There was a dollar and thirty cents in a change jar on her desk. She looked through several purses in the closet, in the coat pockets, a kitchen drawer, until she got together the four dollars that bloody wog charged for a half pint at that hour. All the sick drunks paid him. Although most of them bought sweet wine, it worked quicker.

It was far to walk. It would take her three quarters of an hour; she would have to run home to be there before the kids woke up. Could she make it? She could hardly walk from one room to the other. Just pray a patrol car didn't pass. She wished she had a dog to walk. I know, she laughed, I'll ask the neighbors if I can borrow their dog. Sure. None of the neighbors spoke to her anymore.

It kept her steady to concentrate on the cracks in the sidewalk to count them one two three. Pulling herself along on bushes, tree trunks, like climbing a mountain sideways. Crossing the streets was terrifying, they were so wide, with their lights blinking red red, yellow yellow. An occasional *Examiner* truck, an empty taxi. A police car going fast, without lights. They didn't see her. Cold sweat ran down her back, her teeth chattered loudly in the still dark morning.

She was panting and faint by the time she got to the Uptown on Shattuck. It wasn't open yet. Seven black men, all old except for one young boy, stood outside on the curb. The Indian man sat oblivious to them inside the window, sipping coffee. On the sidewalk two men were sharing a bottle of Nyquil cough syrup. Blue death, you could buy that all night long.

An old man they called Champ smiled at her. "Say, mama, you be sick? Your hair hurt?" She nodded. That's how it felt, your hair, your eyeballs, your bones. "Here," Champ said, "you better eat some of these." He was eating saltines, passed her two. "Gotta make yourself eat." "Say Champ, lemme have a few," the young boy said.

38

Unmanageable

They let her go to the counter first. She asked for vodka and poured her pile of coins onto the counter.

"It's all there," she said.

He smiled, "Count it for me."

"Come on. Shit," the boy said as she counted out the coins with violently shaking hands. She put the bottle into her purse, stumbled toward the door. Outside she held on to a telephone pole, afraid to cross the street.

Champ was drinking from his bottle of Night Train.

"You too much a lady to drink on the street?" She shook her head. "I'm afraid I'll drop the bottle."

"Here," he said. "Open your mouth. You need something or you'll never get home." He poured wine into her mouth. It coursed through her, warm. "Thank you," she said.

She quickly crossed the street, jogged clumsily down the streets toward her house, ninety, ninety-one, counting the cracks. It was still pitch dark when she got to her door.

Gasping for air. Without turning on the light she poured some cranberry juice into a glass, a third of the bottle. She sat down at the table and sipped the drink slowly, the relief of the alcohol seeping throughout her body. She was crying, with relief that she had not died. She poured another third from the bottle and some juice, rested her head on the table between sips.

When she had finished that drink she felt better, and she went into the laundry room and started a load of wash. Taking the bottle with her she went to the bathroom then. She showered and combed her hair, put on clean clothes. Ten more minutes. She checked to see if the door was locked, sat on the toilet and finished the bottle of vodka. This last drink didn't just get her well but got her slightly drunk.

She moved the laundry from the washer to the dryer. She was mixing orange juice from frozen concentrate when Joel came into the kitchen, rubbing his eyes. "No socks, no shirt."

"Hi, honey. Have some cereal. Your clothes will be dry by

the time you finish breakfast and shower." She poured him some juice, another glass for Nicholas who stood silent in the doorway.

"How in the hell did you get a drink?" He pushed past her and poured himself some cereal. Thirteen. He was taller than she.

"Could I have my wallet and keys?" she asked.

"You can have your wallet. I'll give you the keys when I know you're ok."

"I'm ok. I'll be back at work tomorrow."

"You can't stop anymore without a hospital, Ma."

"I'll be fine. Please don't worry. I'll have all day to get well." She went to check the clothes in the dryer.

"The shirts are dry," she told Joel. "The socks need about ten more minutes."

"Can't wait. I'll wear them wet."

Her sons got their books and back packs, kissed her goodbye and went out the door. She stood in the window and watched them go down the street to the bus stop. She waited until the bus picked them up and headed up Telegraph Avenue. She left then, for the liquor store on the corner. It was open now.

Teen-Age Punk

In the sixties, Jesse used to come over to see Ben. They were young kids then, long hair, strobe lights, weed and acid. Jesse had already dropped out of school, already had a probation officer. The Rolling Stones came to New Mexico. The Doors. Ben and Jesse had wept when Jimi Hendrix died, when Janis Joplin died. That was another year for weather. Snow. Frozen pipes. Everybody cried that year.

We lived in an old farmhouse, down by the river. Marty and I had just divorced, I was in my first year of teaching, my first job. The house was hard to take care of alone. Leaky roof, burnt-out pump, but it was big, a beautiful house.

Ben and Jesse played music loud, burned violet incense that smelled of cat pee. My other sons Keith and Nathan couldn't stand Jesse—hippie burnout—but Joel, the baby, adored him, his boots, his guitar, his pellet gun. Beer-can practice in the back yard. Ping.

It was March and cold for sure. The next morning the cranes would be at the clear ditch at dawn. I had learned about them from the new pediatrician. He's a good doctor, and single, but I still miss old Dr. Bass. When Ben was a baby I called him to ask how many diapers I should wash at a time. One, he told me.

None of the kids had wanted to go. I dressed, shivering. Built a piñon fire, poured coffee into a thermos. Fixed batter for pancakes, fed the dogs and cats and Rosie the goat. Did we have a horse then? If so, I forgot to feed him. Jesse came up behind me in the dark, at the barbed wire by the frost-white road.

"I want to see the cranes."

I gave him the flashlight, think I gave him the thermos too. He shined the light everywhere but the road and I kept bugging him about it. Come on. Cut it out.

"You can see. You're walking along. You obviously know the road."

True. The dizzy arcs of light swept into birds' nests in pale winter cottonwoods, pumpkins in Gus's field, prehistoric silhouettes of his Brahmin bulls. Their agate eyes opened to reflect a pinpoint of dazzle, closed again.

We crossed the log above the slow dark irrigation ditch, over to the clear ditch where we lay on our stomachs, silent as guerrillas. I know, I romanticize everything. It is true though that we lay there freezing for a long time in the fog. It was fog. Must have been mist from the ditch or maybe just the steam from our mouths.

After a long time the cranes did come. Hundreds, just as the sky turned blue gray. They landed in slow motion on brittle legs. Washing, preening on the bank. Everything was suddenly black and white and gray, a movie after the credits, churning.

As the cranes drank upstream the silver water beneath them was shot into dozens of thin streamers. Then very quickly the birds left, in whiteness, with the sound of shuffling cards.

We lay there, drinking coffee, until it was light and the crows came. Gawky raucous crows, defying the cranes' grace. Their blackness zigzagged in the water, cottonwood branches bounced like trampolines. You could feel the sun.

It was light on the road back but he left the flashlight on. Turn it off, will you? He ignored me so I took it from him. We walked in his long strides in the tractor tracks.

"Fuck," he said. "That was scary."

"Really. As terrible as an army with banners. That's from the Bible."

"Oh yeah, teacher?" He already had an attitude, then.

Good and Bad

Nuns tried hard to teach me to be good. In high school it was Miss Dawson. Santiago College, 1952. Six of us in the school were going on to American colleges; we had to take American History and Civics from the new teacher, Ethel Dawson. She was the only American teacher, the others were Chilean or European.

We were all bad to her. I was the worst. If there was to be a test and none of us had studied I could distract her with questions about the Gadsden Purchase for the whole period, or get her started on segregation or American imperialism if we were really in trouble.

We mocked her, imitated her nasal Boston whine. She had a tall lift on one shoe because of polio, wore thick wire-rimmed glasses. Splayed gap teeth, a horrible voice. It seemed she deliberately made herself look worse by wearing mannish, mismatched colors, wrinkled, soup-spotted slacks, garish scarves on her badly-cut hair. She got very red-faced when she lectured and she smelled of sweat. It was not simply that she flaunted poverty... Madame Tournier wore the same shabby black skirt and blouse day after day, but the skirt was cut on the bias, the black blouse, green and frayed with age, was of fine silk. Style, cachet were all-important to us then.

She showed us movies and slides about the condition of the Chilean miners and dock workers, all of it the U.S.A.'s fault. The

43

ambassador's daughter was in the class, a few admirals' daughters. My father was a mining engineer, worked with the CIA. I knew he truly believed Chile needed the United States. Miss Dawson thought that she was reaching impressionable young minds, whereas she was talking to spoiled American brats. Each one of us had a rich, handsome, powerful American daddy. Girls feel about their fathers at that age like they do about horses. It is a passion. She implied that they were villains.

Because I did most of the talking I was the one she zeroed in on, keeping me after class, and one day even walked with me in the rose garden, complaining about the elitism of the school. I lost patience with her.

"What are you doing here then? Why don't you go teach the poor if you're so worried about them? Why have anything to do with us snobs at all?"

She told me that this was where she was given work, because she taught American History. She didn't speak Spanish yet, but all her spare time was spent working with the poor and volunteering in revolutionary groups. She said it wasn't a waste of time working with us . . . if she could change the thinking of one mind it would be worthwhile.

"Perhaps you are that one mind," she said. We sat on a stone bench. Recess was almost over. Scent of roses and the mildew of her sweater.

"Tell me, what do you do with your weekends?" she asked.

It wasn't hard to sound utterly frivolous, but I exaggerated it anyway. Hairdresser, manicurist, dressmaker. Lunch at the Charles. Polo, rugby or cricket, *thés dansants*, dinners, parties until dawn. Mass at El Bosque at seven on Sunday morning, still wearing evening clothes. The country club then for breakfast, golf or swimming, or maybe the day in Algarrobo at the sea, skiing in winter. Movies of course, but mostly we danced all night.

"And this life is satisfying to you?" she asked.

"Yes. It is."

Good and Bad

"What if I asked you to give me your Saturdays, for one month, would you do it? See a part of Santiago that you don't know."

"Why do you want me?"

"Because, basically, I think you are a good person. I think you could learn from it." She clasped both my hands. "Give it a try."

Good person. But she had caught me earlier, with the word Revolutionary. I did want to meet revolutionaries, because they were bad.

Everyone seemed a lot more upset than necessary about my Saturdays with Miss Dawson, which then made me really want to do it. I told my mother I was going to help the poor. She was disgusted, afraid of disease, toilet seats. I even knew that the poor in Chile had no toilet seats. My friends were shocked that I was going with Miss Dawson at all. They said she was a loony, a fanatic, and a lesbian, was I crazy or what?

The first day I spent with her was ghastly, but I stuck with it out of bravado.

Every Saturday morning we went to the city dump, in a pickup truck filled with huge pots of food. Beans, porridge, biscuits, milk. We set up a big table in a field next to miles of shacks made from flattened tin cans. A bent water faucet about three blocks away served the entire shack community. There were open fires in front of the squalid lean-tos, burning scraps of wood, cardboard, shoes, to cook on.

At first the place seemed to be deserted, miles and miles of dunes. Dunes of stinking, smouldering garbage. After a while, through the dust and smoke, you could see that there were people all over the dunes. But they were the color of the dung, their rags just like the refuse they crawled in. No one stood up, they scurried on all fours like wet rats, tossing things into burlap bags that gave them humped animal backs, circling on, darting, meeting each other, touching noses, slithering away, disappearing like iguanas over the ridges of the dunes. But once the food was set up scores of women and children appeared,

45

sooty and wet, smelling of decay and rotted food. They were glad for the breakfast, squatted, eating with bony elbows out like preying mantis on the garbage hills. After they had eaten, the children crowded around me; still crawling or sprawled in the dirt, they patted my shoes, ran their hands up and down my stockings.

"See, they like you," Miss Dawson said. "Doesn't that make you feel good?"

I knew that they liked my shoes and stockings, my red Chanel jacket.

Miss Dawson and her friends were exhilarated as we drove away, chatting happily. I was sickened and depressed.

"What good does it do to feed them once a week. It doesn't make a dent in their lives. They need more than biscuits once a week, for lord's sake."

Right. But until the revolution came and everything was shared you had to do whatever helped at all.

"They need to know somebody realizes they live out here. We tell them that soon things will change. Hope. It's about hope," Miss Dawson said.

We had lunch in a tenement in the south of the city, Six flights up. One window that looked on to an airshaft. A hot plate, no running water. Any water they used had to be carried up those stairs. The table was set with four bowls and four spoons, a pile of bread in the center. There were many people, talking in small groups. I spoke Spanish, but they spoke in a heavy *caló* with almost no consonants, and were hard for me to understand. They ignored us, looked at us with amused tolerance or complete disdain. I didn't hear revolutionary talk, but talk about work, money, filthy jokes. We all took turns eating lentils, drinking *chicha*, a raw wine, using the same bowls and glass as the person before.

"Nice you don't seem to mind about dirt," beamed Miss Dawson.

Good and Bad

"I grew up in mining towns. Lots of dirt." But the cabins of Finnish and Basque miners were pretty, with flowers and candles, sweet-faced Virgins. This was an ugly, filthy place with misspelled slogans on the walls, communist pamphlets stuck up with chewing gum. There was a newspaper photograph of my father and the minister of mines, splattered with blood.

"Hey!" I said. Miss Dawson took my hand, stroked it. "Sh," she said in English. "We're on first name basis here. Don't for heaven's sake say who you are. Now, Adele, don't be uncomfortable. To grow up you need to face all the realities of your father's personae."

"Not with blood on them."

"Precisely that way. It is a strong possibility and you should be aware of it." She squeezed both my hands then.

After lunch she took me to "El Niño Perdido," an orphanage in an old stone ivy-covered building in the foothills of the Andes. It was run by French nuns, lovely old nuns, with fleur-de-lis coifs and blue-grey habits. They floated through the dark rooms, above the stone floors, flew down the passages by the flowered courtyard, popped open wooden shutters, calling out in bird-like voices. They brushed away insane children who were biting their legs, dragging them by their little feet. They washed ten faces in a row, all the eyes blind. They fed six mongoloid giants, reaching up with spoons of oatmeal.

These orphans all had something the matter. Some were insane, others had no legs or were mute, some had been burned over their entire bodies. No noses or ears. Syphilitic babies and mongoloids in their teens. The assorted afflictions spilled together from room to room, out into the courtyard into the lovely unkempt garden.

"There are many things needed to do," Miss Dawson said. "I like feeding and changing babies. You might read to the blind children...they all seem particularly intelligent and bored."

There were few books. La Fontaine in Spanish. They sat in a

circle, staring at me, really blankly. Nervous, I began a game, a clapping and stomping kind of game like musical chairs. They liked that and so did some other children.

I hated the dump on Saturdays but I liked going to the orphanage. I even liked Miss Dawson when we were there. She spent her time bathing and rocking babies and singing to them, while I made up games for the older children. Some things worked and others didn't. Relay races didn't because nobody would let go of the stick. Jump rope was great because two boys with Down's syndrome would turn the rope for hours on end without stopping, while everybody, especially the blind girls, took turns. Even nuns jumped, jump jump they hovered blue in the air. Farmer in the Dell. Button Button. Hide-and-go-seek didn't work because nobody came home. The orphans were glad to see me; I loved going there, not because I was good, but because I liked to play.

Saturday nights we went to revolutionary theatre or poetry readings. We heard the greatest Latin American poets of our century. These were poets whose work I would later love, whom I would study and teach. But then I did not listen. I suffered an agony of self-consciousness and confusion. We were the only Americans there; all I heard were the attacks against the United States. Many people asked questions about American policy that I couldn't answer; I referred them to Miss Dawson and translated her answers, ashamed and baffled by what I told them, about segregation, Anaconda. She didn't realize how much the people scorned us, how they mocked her banal communist clichés about their reality. They laughed at me with my Josef haircut and nails, my expensive casual clothes. At one theatre group they put me on stage and the director hollered, "OK *Gringa*, tell me why you are in my country!" I froze and sat down, to hooting and laughter. Finally I told Miss Dawson I couldn't go out on Saturday nights anymore.

Dinner and dancing at Marcelo Errazuriz's. Martinis, consommé in little cups on the terrace, fragrant gardens beyond us. A six course dinner that began at eleven. Everyone teased me about my days with Miss Dawson, begged me to tell them where I went. I couldn't talk about it, not with my friends nor my parents. I remember someone making a joke about me and my *rotos*, "broken" meant poor people then. I felt ashamed, aware that there were almost as many servants in the room as guests.

I joined Miss Dawson in a workers' protest outside the United States Embassy. I had only walked about a block when a friend of my father's, Frank Wise, grabbed me out of the crowd, took me to the Crillon Hotel.

He was furious. "What in God's name do you think you are doing?" He soon understood what Miss Dawson didn't . . . that I had not the faintest idea of politics, of what any of this was about. He told me that it would be terrible for my father if the press found out what I was doing. I understood that.

On another Saturday afternoon I agreed to stand downtown and collect money for the orphanage. I stood on one corner and Miss Dawson on another. In only a few minutes dozens of people had insulted and cursed me. I didn't understand, shifted my sign for "Give to El Niño Perdido," and rattled the cup. Tito and Pepe, two friends, were on their way to the Waldorf for coffee. They whisked me away, forced me to go with them to coffee.

"This is *not* done here. Poor people beg. You are insulting the poor. For a woman to solicit anything gives a shocking image. You will destroy your reputation. Also no one would believe you are not keeping the money. A girl simply can't stand on the street unescorted. You can go to charity balls or luncheons, but physical contact with other classes is simply vulgar, and patronizing to them. Also you absolutely cannot afford to be seen with someone of her sexual persuasion in public. My dear, you are too young, you don't understand. . . ."

We drank Jamaican coffee and I listened to them. I told them I saw what they were saying but I couldn't just leave Miss Dawson alone on the corner. They said they would speak to her. The three of us went down Ahumada to where she stood, proudly, while passersby muttered *"Gringa loca"* or *"puta coja,"* crippled whore, at her.

"It is not appropriate, in Santiago, for a young girl to do this, and we are taking her home," was all Tito said to her. She looked at him with disdain, and later that week, in the hallway at school she told me it was wrong to let men dictate my actions. I told her that I felt everybody dictated my actions, that I had gone with her on Saturdays a month longer than I had first promised. That I wasn't going any more.

"It is wrong for you to return to a totally selfish existence. To fight for a better world is the only reason for living. Have you learned nothing?"

"I learned a lot. I see that many things need to change. But it's their struggle, not mine."

"I can't believe you can say that. Don't you see, that's what is wrong with the world, that attitude."

She limped crying to the bathroom, was late to class, where she told us there would be no class that day. The six of us went out and lay on the grass in the gardens, away from the windows so no one could see that we weren't in class. The girls teased me, said that I was breaking Miss Dawson's heart. She was obviously in love with me. Did she try to kiss me? This really made me confused and mad. In spite of everything I was beginning to like her, her dogged naive commitment, her hopefulness. She was like a little kid, like one of the blind children when they gasped with pleasure, playing in the water sprinkler. Miss Dawson never flirted with me or tried to touch me all the time like boys did. But she wanted me to do things I didn't want to do and I felt like a bad person for not wanting to, for not caring more about the injustice in the world. The girls got mad at me because I wouldn't talk about her. They called me Miss Dawson's mistress. There was nobody I could talk to about any of this, nobody to ask what was right or wrong, so I just felt wrong.

Good and Bad

It was windy my last day at the dump. Sand sifted into the porridge in glistening waves. When the figures rose on the hills it was with a swirl of dirt so they looked like silver ghosts, dervishes. None of them had shoes and their feet crept silently over the soggy mounds. They didn't speak, or shout to each other, like most people do who work together, and they never spoke to us. Beyond the steaming dung hills was the city and above us all the white Andes. They ate. Miss Dawson didn't say a word, gathering up the pots and utensils in the sigh of wind.

We had agreed to go to a farm workers' rally outside of town that afternoon. We ate *churrascos* on the street, stopped by her apartment for her to change.

Her apartment was dingy and airless. The fact that her hot plate for cooking was on the toilet tank made me feel ill, as did the odor of old wool and sweat and hair. She changed in front of me, which I found shocking and frightening, her naked, distorted blue-white body. She put on a sleeveless sundress with no brassiere.

"Miss Dawson, that would be all right at night, in someone's home, or at the beach, but you just can't go around bare like that in Chile."

"I pity you. All your life you are going to be paralyzed by What Is Done, by what people tell you you should think or do. I do not dress to please others. It is a very hot day, and I feel comfortable in this dress."

"Well...it makes me not comfortable. People will say rude things to us. It is different here, from the United States..."

"The best thing that could happen to you would be for you to be uncomfortable once in a while."

We took several crowded busses to get to the *fundo* where the rally was, waiting in the hot sun and standing on the busses. We got down and walked down a beautiful lane lined with eucalyptus, stopped to cool off in the stream by the lane.

We had arrived too late for the speeches. There was an empty platform, a banner with "Land Back to the People" hanging askew behind the mike. There was a small group of men in suits, obviously the organizers, but most of the people were farm laborers. Guitars were playing and there was a crowd around a couple dancing *La Cueca* in a desultory fashion, languidly waving handkerchiefs as they circled one another. People were pouring wine from huge vats or standing in line for spit-roasted beef and beans. Miss Dawson told me to find us a place at one of the tables, that she would bring our food.

I squeezed into a spot at the end of a table crowded with families. Nobody was talking politics, it seemed that these were just country people who had come to a free barbeque. Everyone was very, very drunk. I could see Miss Dawson, chattering away in line, she was drinking wine too, gesticulating and talking very loud so people would understand her.

"Isn't this great?" she asked, bringing two huge plates of food. "Let's introduce ourselves. Try to talk to the people more, that's how you learn, and help."

The two farm workers we sat by decided with gales of laughter that we were from another planet. As I had feared, they were amazed by her bare shoulders and visible nipples, couldn't figure out what she was. I realized that not only did she not speak Spanish, she was nearly blind. She would squint through her inch-thick glasses, smiling, but she couldn't see that these men were laughing at us, didn't like us, whatever we were. What were we doing here? She tried to explain that she was in the communist party, but instead of *partido* she kept toasting the *"Fiesta,"* which is a festive party, so they kept toasting her back, "La Fiesta!"

"We've got to leave," I said, but she only looked at me, slack-jawed and drunk. The man next to me was half-heartedly flirting with me, but I was more worried about the big drunk man next to Miss Dawson. He was stroking her shoulders with one hand while he ate a rib with the other. She was laughing away until he started grabbing her and kissing her, then she began to scream.

Miss Dawson ended up on the ground, sobbing uncontrollably. Everyone had rushed over at first, but they soon left, muttering "Nothing but some drunken *gringa*." The men we had sat by now ignored us totally. She got up and began to run toward the road; I followed her. When she got to the stream she tried to wash herself off, her mouth and her chest. She just got muddy and wet. She sat on the bank, crying, her nose running. I gave her my handkerchief.

"Miss Perfect! An ironed linen handkerchief!" she sneered.

"Yes." I said, fed up with her and only concerned now with getting home. Still crying, she staggered down the path toward the main road, where she started to hail down cars. I pulled her back into the trees.

"Look, Miss Dawson. You can't hitchhike here. They don't understand . . . it could get us in trouble, two women hitchhiking. Listen to me!"

But a farmer in an old truck had stopped, the engine ticking on the dusty road. I offered him money to take us to the outskirts of town. He was going all the way to downtown, could take us all the way to her house easy for 20 pesos. We climbed into the bed of the truck.

She put her arms around me in the wind. I could feel her wet dress, her sticky armpit hairs as she clung to me.

"You can't go back to your frivolous life! Don't leave! Don't leave me," she kept saying until at last we got to her block.

"Goodbye," I said. "Thanks for everything," or something dumb like that. I left her on the curb, blinking at my cab until it turned the corner.

The maids were leaning on the gate talking to the neighborhood *carabinero*, so I didn't think anyone was home. But my father was there, changing to go play golf.

"You're back early. Where have you been?" he asked.

"To a picnic, with my history teacher."

"Oh, yes. What is she like?"

"OK. She's a communist."

I just blurted that out. It had been a miserable day; I was fed up with Miss Dawson. But that's all it took. Three words to my father. She was fired sometime that weekend and we never saw her again.

No one else knew what had happened. The other girls were happy she was gone. We had a free period now, even though we would have to make up American history when we got to college. There was nobody to speak to. To say I was sorry.

Grief

"Whatever can those two be talking about all the time?" Mrs. Wacher asked her husband at breakfast.

Across the open-air, thatched-roof dining room by the sea the sisters forgot their papaya, their *huevos rancheros*, talking, talking. Later, as they walked by the edge of the sea, their heads were bent toward one another. Talking, talking. Waves would catch them unawares, soaking them, and they would laugh. The younger one often cried . . . When she cried the older one waited, comforting her, passing her a tissue. When the tears stopped they began talking again. She didn't look hard, the older one, but she never cried.

《 · 》

For the most part the other hotel guests in the dining room and in beach chairs on the sand all sat quietly together, occasionally commenting upon the perfection of the day, the turquoise blue of the sea, telling their children to sit up straight. The honeymoon couple whispered and teased each other, fed one another bites of melon, but most of the time they were silent, gazing into the other's eyes, looking at the other's hands. The older couples drank coffee and read or did crossword puzzles. Their conversations were brief, monosyllabic. The people who were content with each other spoke as little as those who bristled with resentment or boredom; it was the rhythm of their speech that differed, like a lazy tennis ball batted back and forth or the quick swattings of a fly.

« · »

In the evening, by lantern light, the German couple, the Wachers, played bridge with another retired couple from Canada, the Lewises. They were all serious players so there was a minimum of conversation. Snap snap of dealt cards, Mr. Wacher's "hmms." Two no trump. The sizzle of the surf, ice cubes in their glasses. The women spoke, occasionally, about plans for shopping the next day, a trip to La Isla, the mysterious talking sisters. The older one so elegant and cool. In her fifties but still attractive, vain. The younger one, in her forties, was pretty, but frumpy, self-effacing. There she goes, crying again!

Mrs. Wacher decided to tackle the older sister during her morning swim. Mrs. Lewis would speak to the younger one, who never swam or sat in the sun, but waited for the other, sipping tea, holding an unopened book.

« · »

That evening, while Mr. Wacher fetched the score pad and cards and Mr. Lewis ordered drinks and snacks from the bar, the two women pooled their information.

"They talk so much because they haven't seen each other in twenty years! Can you imagine? Sisters? Mine is named Sally, she lives in Mexico City, is married to a Mexican and has three children. We spoke in Spanish, she seems Mexican really. She recently had a mastectomy, which explains why she doesn't swim. She starts cancer therapy next month. That's probably why she's crying all the time. That's all I got, before the sister came up and they went to change."

Grief

"No! That's not why she's crying! Their mother has just died! Two weeks ago! Can you imagine...they have come to a resort?"

"What else did she say? What is her name?"

"Dolores. She is a nurse from California, with four grown sons. She said that their mother recently died, that she and her sister had a lot to talk about."

The women figured it all out. Sally, the sweet one, must have been taking care of the invalid mother all these years. When the old mother finally died Dolores felt guilty, because of her sister caring for her mother, and she never went to visit them. And then her sister's cancer. Dolores was the one paying for everything, the cabs, the waiters. They saw her buying Sally clothes in the boutiques downtown. That must be it. Guilt. She's sorry she didn't see her mother before she died, wants to be good to her sister before she dies too.

"Or before she dies herself," Mrs. Lewis said. "When your parents are dead your own death faces you."

"Oh, I know what you mean...there is no one to protect you against death anymore."

The two women were silent then, pleased with their harmless gossip, their analysis. Thinking of their own deaths to come. Their husbands' deaths to come. But just briefly. Although in their seventies both couples were healthy, active. They lived fully, enjoying each day. When their husbands pulled out their chairs and sat down for the game they entered it with pleasure, forgetting all about the two sisters, who were sitting side by side now on the beach, under the stars.

« · »

Sally wasn't crying about their dead mother or her cancer. She was crying because her husband Alfonso had left her, after twenty years, for a young woman. It seemed a brutal thing to do, just after her mastectomy. She was devastated, but no she

57

wouldn't ever divorce him, even though the woman was pregnant and he wanted to marry her.

"They can just wait until I die. I'll be dead soon, probably next year..." Sally wept but the ocean drowned out the sound.

"You're not dying. They said the cancer was gone. The radiation therapy is routine, a precaution. I heard the doctor say that, that they got all the cancer."

"But it will come back. It always does."

"That's not true. Cut it out, Sally."

"You are so cold. Sometimes you are as cruel as Mama."

Dolores said nothing. Her greatest fear, that she was like her mother. Cruel, a drunkard.

"Look, Sally. Just give him a divorce and start taking care of yourself."

"You don't understand! How can you understand how I feel after living with him for twenty years? You've been alone almost that long! For me it has only been Alfonso, since I was seventeen! I love him!"

"I think I can manage to understand," Dolores said, dryly. "Come on, let's go in, it's getting cold."

« · »

In the room Dolores' light was on inside her white mosquito net; she was reading before she fell asleep.

"Dolores?"

Sally was crying, again. Christ. Now what.

"Sally, I go crazy if I can't read when I first wake up and before I go to sleep. It's a dumb habit, but there it is. What is it?"

"I have a splinter in my foot."

Dolores got up, went for a needle, some antiseptic and a band-aid, removed the splinter from her sister's foot. Sally cried again, and embraced Dolores.

Grief

"Let's always be close now. It's so good to have a sister who takes care of me!"

Dolores smoothed the band-aid on Sally's foot, as she had done a dozen times when they were children. "All better," she said, automatically.

"All better!" Sally sighed. She fell asleep soon after. Dolores read for several hours more. Finally she turned out the light, wishing she had a drink.

How could she talk to Sally about her alcoholism? It was not like talking about a death, or losing a husband, losing a breast. People said it was a disease, but nobody made her pick up the drink. I've got a fatal disease. I am terrified, Dolores wanted to say, but she didn't.

《 · 》

The Wachers and the Lewises were always the first people up for breakfast, seated at adjoining tables. The husbands read the paper, the wives chatted with the waiters and one another. After breakfast the four were going out deep-sea fishing.

"Where are the sisters today, I wonder?" Mrs. Lewis said.

"Hollering! When I passed their room they were arguing away. Herman has no compassion, he wouldn't let me eaves-drop. Sally said, No! She didn't want a penny of the old witch's blood money! That when she had been desperate her mother had refused her, cussing away, that meek little thing! *Puta! Desgraciada!* Dolores was hollering at her, 'Can't you understand anything about madness? *You* are the really crazy one... because you refuse to see! Mama was crazy!' And then she began yelling at her, 'Take it off! Take it off!'"

"Shh. Here they come now."

Sally was disheveled; she looked, as usual, as if she had been weeping; as usual Dolores was calm and perfectly groomed.

59

So Long: Stories

She ordered breakfast for the two of them and when it came you could hear her say to her sister,

"Eat. You'll feel better. Drink all the orange juice. It is sweet, delicious."

« · »

"Take it off!"

Sally cowered, clutching her *huipil* to her body. Dolores tore it away from her, made her stand there, naked, the scars where her breast had been livid red and blue.

Sally cried. "I am hideous! I'm not a woman now! Don't look!"

Dolores gripped her shoulders, shook her. "You want me to be your sister? Let me look! Yes, it is hideous. The scars look brutal, awful. But they are you now. And you're a woman, you silly fool! Without your Alfonso, without your breast, you can be more of a woman than ever, your own woman! For starters you're going swimming today, with that $150 falsie I brought to pin in your suit."

"I can't."

"Yes you can. Come on, get dressed for breakfast."

« · »

"Good morning, ladies!" Mrs. Lewis called to the sisters. "Another splendid day. We're going fishing. What are your plans for the day?"

"We're going for a swim, and then shopping and to the hairdresser."

"Poor Sally," Mrs. Lewis said, "She obviously doesn't want to do any of those things. She's sick, and grieving. That sister of hers is forcing her to be on vacation. Just like my sister Iris. Bossy, bossy! Did you have a big sister?"

"No," Mrs. Wacher laughed. "I was the big sister. Believe me, little sisters have their drawbacks too."

Grief

Dolores spread out their towels on the sand.

"Take it off."

She meant the robe her sister had clutched over her bathing suit.

"Take it off," she insisted again. "You look wonderful. Your breast looks real. Your waist is tiny. You have great legs. But then you never, ever, realized how lovely you were."

"No. You were the pretty one. I was the good one."

"That label was hard on me too. Take the hat off. We only have a few days left. You're going back to the city with a tan."

"*Pero...*"

"*Callate.* Keep your mouth shut, so you don't tan with wrinkles."

« · »

"The sun feels wonderful," Sally sighed after a while.

"Doesn't your body feel good?"

"I feel so naked. As if everyone could see the scars."

"You know one thing I've learned? Most people don't notice anything at all, or care, if they do."

"You are so cynical."

"Turn over, let me oil your back."

After a while Sally talked to Dolores about the library in the *barrio* where she worked as a volunteer. Heartwarming stories about the children and families who lived in dire poverty. She loved her work there, and they loved her.

"See, Sally, there is so much you can do, that you enjoy."

Dolores couldn't think of any heartwarming stories to tell Sally about her job, at a clinic in East Oakland. Crack babies, abused children, children with brain damage, Down's syndrome, gun-shot wounds, malnutrition, AIDS. But she was good at her job, and liked it. Or had—she had finally been fired for drinking, just last month, before their mother died.

"I like my job, too," was all she said. "Come on, let's swim."
"I can't. I'll hurt myself."
"The wounds are healed, Sally. There are only scars. Terrible scars."
"I can't."
"For Christ's sake, get in the water."

Dolores led her sister into the surf and then wrenched her hand away. She watched Sally flounder and fall, swallow water, be knocked down by a wave. Treading water she watched as Sally stood up and dove under the incoming swell, swam on. Dolores swam after her. Oh Lord, she's crying again, but no, Sally was laughing out loud.

"It's warm! It's so warm! I'm light as a baby!"

They swam out in the blue water for a long time. At last they came in to shore. Breathless, laughing, they left the surf. Sally threw her arms around her sister and the two women held each other, the foam swirling around their ankles. *"Mariconas!"* mocked two passing beach boys.

« · »

Mrs. Lewis and Mrs. Wacher watched from their beach chairs, quite moved. "She's not so mean, just firm . . . she knew the sister would like it once she got in. How happy she looks. Poor thing, she needed this vacation."

"Yes, it doesn't seem so shocking now, does it? That they should go on a holiday when their mother died."

"You know . . . it's too bad it isn't a tradition. A post-funeral holiday, like a honeymoon, or a baby shower."

They both laughed. "Herman!" Mrs. Wacher called over to her husband. "After we two women have died, will you two men promise to take a vacation together?"

Herman shook his head. "No. You need four for bridge."

Grief

When Sally and Dolores got back that evening everyone com-
plimented Sally on how lovely she looked. Rosy from the sun,
her new haircut curling in soft auburn ringlets around her face.

Sally kept shaking her hair, looking in the mirror. Her green
eyes shone like emeralds. She was painting them with Dolores's
makeup.

"Could I borrow your green top?" she asked.

"What? I just bought you three beautiful dresses. Now you
want my top? And for that matter you have your own makeup,
and your own perfume!"

"See how you resent me! Yes, you give me presents, but you
still are selfish, selfish, like her!"

"Selfish!" Dolores took her blouse off. "Here! Take these ear-
rings, too. They go with it."

« · »

The sun set as the diners ate their flan. When their coffee came
Dolores reached for her sister's hand.

"You realize we're just acting as we did when we were chldren.
It's sort of nice when you think about it. You keep saying that
you want us to be real sisters now. We're acting just like real
sisters! Fighting!"

Sally smiled. "You're right. I guess I never knew how real
families acted. We never had a family vacation, or even a picnic."

"I'm sure that's why I had so many children, why you married
into such a huge Mexican family, we wanted a home so badly."

"And that's just why Alfonso leaving me is so hard..."

"Don't talk about him anymore."

"What can I talk about then?"

"We need to talk about her. Mama. She's dead now."

So Long: Stories

"I could have killed her! I'm glad she's dead," Sally said. "It was too awful when Daddy died. I flew to L.A. and took a bus to San Clemente. She wouldn't even let me in the door. I banged on the door and said, 'I need a mother! Let me talk to you!' but she wouldn't let me in. It wasn't fair. I don't care about the money, but that wasn't fair either."

Their mother had never forgiven Sally for marrying a Mexican, had refused to meet her children, left her money to Dolores. Dolores insisted upon dividing the inheritance, but it didn't lessen the insult.

Dolores rocked Sally as they sat on the sand. The sun had set.

"She's gone, Sally. She was sick, afraid. She lashed out, like a wounded . . . hyena. You're lucky you didn't see her. I saw her. I called her to say we were taking Daddy to the hospital by ambulance. You know what she said? 'Could you stop and pick up some bananas?'"

《 · 》

"Today is my last day!" Sally said to Mrs. Wacher. "We're going to the island. Have you ever been?"

"Oh, yes, we went with the Lewises a few days ago. It's perfectly lovely. You're going snorkeling?"

"Scuba," Dolores said. "*Vamos*, Sally, the car is waiting."

"I'm not going scuba diving. That's it," Sally said on the way to Ixtapa.

"You'll see. Wait until you meet César. I lived with him awhile, twenty-five, thirty years ago. He was just a diver then, a fisherman."

He had become famous and rich since then, the Jacques Cousteau of Mexico, with many movies, television programs. This was hard for Dolores to imagine. She remembered his old wooden boat, the sand floor of his *palapa*, their hammock.

"He was a maestro even then," she said. "Nobody knows the

64

Grief

ocean like he does. His press releases call him Neptune, and that sounds pretty corny... but it's true. He probably won't remember me, but I still want you to meet him."

« · »

He was an old man now, with a long white beard, flowing white hair. Of course he remembered Dolores. Sweet his kiss on her eyelids, his embrace. She remembered his calloused, scarred hands on her skin. . . . He led them to a table on the veranda. Two men from the Tourist Bureau were drinking tequila, fanning themselves with their straw hats, their *guayaberas* damp and wrinkled.

The vast veranda faced the ocean, but mango and avocado trees totally blocked the ocean from sight.

"How can you cover up such a view of the ocean?" Sally asked.

César shrugged, *"Pues,* I've seen it."

He told them all about dives he and Dolores had been on years ago. The time with the sharks, the giant *peine,* the day Flaco drowned. How the divers used to call her "La Brava." But she scarcely heard his praise of her. She heard him say, "When she was young she was a beautiful woman."

"So, have you come to dive with me?" he asked, holding her hands. She longed to dive; she couldn't bear to tell him she was afraid the regulator would break her false teeth.

"No. My back is bad now. I brought my sister to dive with you."

"Lista?" he asked Sally. She was drinking tequila, basking in the compliments and flirtations from the men. The men left. Cesar, Sally and Dolores set out in a canoe to La Isla. Sally gripped the side of the boat, ashen with fear. At one point she leaned over the side, vomiting.

"Are you sure she should dive?" Cesar asked Dolores.

"I'm sure."

They smiled at each other. The years were erased, their communication still there. She had once said wryly that he had been perfect. He couldn't read or write and most of their romance was underwater, where there were no words. There had never been any need for explanations.

Quietly he showed the basics of diving to Sally. At first, out in the shallow water, Sally was still shaking with fear. Dolores sat on the rocks and watched, watched him clean her mask with spit, explain the regulator. He put the tank on her back. Dolores saw Sally stiffen, afraid he would notice her breast, but then she saw Sally unbend, swaying in rhythm before him as he reassured her, fastened her gear and stroked her, soothed her down into the water.

It took four tries. Sally surfaced, choking. No, no it was impossible, she was claustrophobic, couldn't breathe! But he continued to speak softly to her, to coax her, smooth her with his hands. Dolores felt a sick wave of jealousy when he held her sister's head in his hands, smiling into her eyes through their masks. She remembered his smile through the glass.

This was your big idea, she told herself. She tried to be calm, gazing out at the undulating green waves where her sister and César had disappeared. She tried to concentrate upon her sister's pleasure. For she knew it would be pleasure. But all she could feel was regret and remorse, unspeakable loss.

It seemed like hours before they surfaced. Sally was laughing; her laughter was that of a young girl. Impetuously she was kissing and hugging César while he undid her tanks, took off her flippers.

In the diver's hut she embraced Dolores, too. "You knew how great it would be! I flew! The ocean went on forever! Dolores, I felt so alive and strong! I was an Amazon!"

Dolores wanted to point out that Amazons had only one breast, but she bit her tongue. She and César smiled as Sally continued to talk about the beauty of the dive. She'd come back,

Grief

soon, spend a week diving! Oh, the coral and the anemones, the colors, the brilliant schools of fish.

César asked them to lunch. It was three o'clock. "I'm afraid I need a siesta," Dolores said. Sally was disappointed.

"You'll be back, Sally. I just showed you the way."

"Thank you both," Sally said. Her joy and gratitude were pure, innocent. César and her sister kissed her glowing cheeks.

They were at the cab stand on the beach. César held Dolores's hand tightly. "So, *mi vieja*, will you ever come back?" She shook her head.

"Stay with me tonight."

"*No puedo.*"

César kissed her lips. She tasted the desire and salt of their past. The last night she had spent with him he had bitten all her fingernails to the quick. "Think of me," he said.

Sally talked excitedly all the way into town, an hour's drive. How vital she had felt, how free.

"I knew you would like that part. Your body disappears, because you are so weightless, but at the same time you become intensely aware of it."

"He is wonderful. Wonderful. I can just imagine having a love affair with him! You are so lucky!"

"Can you imagine, Sally. That whole stretch of beach, where the Club Med is? It was pure empty beach. Up in the jungle there was an artesian well. There were deer, almost tame. We spent days there without seeing another soul. And the island. It was just an island, wild jungle. No dive shops or restaurants. Not a single other boat but ours. Can you imagine?"

No. She couldn't.

« · »

"It's uncanny," Mrs. Wacher said, as the sisters got down from their cab. "It's as if they have totally reversed roles. Now the

67

younger one is absolutely gorgeous and radiant and the other is haggard and disheveled. Look at her...she who never used to have a hair out of place!"

<< · >>

The night was stormy. Black clouds swept across the full moon so that the beach was bright and then dark, like a hotel room with a neon sign blinking outside. Sally's face shone like a child's when the moonlight lit her.

"But did Mama never, ever, speak of me?"

No, matter of fact. Except to mock your sweetness, to say your docility proved that you were a fool.

"Yes, she did, a lot," Dolores lied. "One of her favorite memories of you was how you loved that Dr. Bunny book. You would pretend to read it, turning the pages, real serious. And you got every word perfect, except when Dr. Bunny would say, 'Case dismissed!' you said 'Smith to Smith!'"

"I remember that book! The rabbits were all furry!"

"At first. But you wore the fur out petting them. She liked to remember you and that red wagon, too, when you were around four. You'd put Billy Jameson in the wagon, and all your dolls, and Mabel, the dog, and the two cats, and then you'd say 'All aboard!' but the cats and dog would have gotten out and Billy too, and the dolls fell out. You'd spend all morning packing them up and saying all aboard."

"I don't remember that at all."

"Oh, I do, it was in the path by Daddy's hyacinths, and the climbing rose by the gate. Can you remember the smell?"

"Yes!"

"She used to ask me if I remembered you in Chile, going off to school on your bicycle. Every single morning you'd look up to the hall window and wave, and your straw hat would fly off."

Grief

Sally laughed. "True. I remember. But, Dolores, it was you in the hall window. You I was waving goodbye to."

True. "Well, I guess she used to see you from the window by her bed."

"Silly how good that makes me feel. I mean even if she didn't ever say goodbye. That she even watched me go off to school. I'm so glad you told me about that."

"Good," Dolores whispered, to herself. The sky was black now and huge raindrops were falling cold. The sisters ran together in the rain to their room.

《 · 》

Sally's plane left the next morning; Dolores would leave the following day. At breakfast, before she left, Sally said goodbye to everyone, thanked the waiters, thanked Mrs. Lewis and Mrs. Wacher for being so kind.

"We're glad that you two had such a good visit. What a comfort to have a sister!" Mrs. Lewis said.

"It really is a comfort," Sally said when she kissed Dolores goodbye at the airport.

"We're just beginning to know each other," Dolores said. "We will be there now, always, for each other." Her heart ached to see the sweetness, the trust in her sister's eyes.

On the way back to the hotel she had the cab stop at a liquor store. In her room she drank and she slept and then she sent out for another bottle. In the morning, on the way to her plane for California she bought a half-pint of rum, to cure her shakes and headache. By the time the taxi reached the airport she was, like they say, feeling no pain.

Daughters

The courage of my own convictions? I can't even hold a per-
ception for longer than five minutes. Just like the radio in a
pick-up truck. I'll be barreling along...Waylon Jennings, Stevie
Wonder... hit a cattleguard & bang it's a preacher from Clint,
Texas. Your laff is trash. Laugh? Life? From one day to the next
the 40 bus alters. Some days there will be people on it from
Chaucer, Damon Runyon. A Breughel feast. I feel close to them
all, at one with them. We are a vivid tapestry of riders, then
there is an epidemic of Giles de la Tourette syndrome and we're
all victims, trapped in a steamy capsule, forever. Sometimes
everyone is tired. Whole bus plumb wore out. Heavy shopping
bags. Cumbersome carts, strollers. Panting up the steps, sleeping past their stops, the people slump, they sway limp from the
poles like languorous seaweed. Or everyone has growth on their
heads. Row after row, and standing, packed, they all have hair
growing out of their heads. Not green willow or eucalyptus or
moss but a billion strands, filaments of hair. Punk hair, blue lady
hair, wet afro hair. Ach, the man in front of me has no hair at
all. He doesn't even have any tiny little holes in his head for it
to come out of. I feel faint. A little girl gets on the bus, wearing
a St. Ignatius uniform. Someone, a grandmother *hold still now
child* has plaited her hair into braids so tight her eyes slant.
The braids are tied with white bows, real satin ribbons. She sits
behind the driver. The morning sun gleams on her perfect part,

makes a halo behind her head. I love the child's hair. I touch my own, pat my own hair which is short and rough, like a Samoyed's or a Chow's. Good boy. Kill, white fang.

I should have taken that job stringing graduated pearls. Working for a doctor, well it's life or death all day long. I glide around, a real angel of mercy. Or a ghoul. Mmmm, Dr. B... interesting, these bone marrow results on Mr. Morbido. That's his name, honest. Truth is weirder than my imagination which really goes berserk with the dialysis machines. Breakthroughs in modern medicine. Life savers that by late afternoon turn into headless plastic vampires, draining blood away. The patients get paler and paler. The machines make a humming sucking sound with an occasional slurp that sounds like a laugh.

By late afternoon I'm ready to strangle Riva Chirenko's daughter. I don't know her name. Nobody calls her Mrs. Tomanovich. She's Mr. Tomanovich's wife. Riva's daughter. Irena Tomanovich's mother. She's what's wrong with all us women, that schleppe from the steppe. But at other times it is this same woman, Riva Chirenko's daughter, that I respect, revere. If I could only accept as she has done, just accept. Acceptance is faith, Henry Miller said. I could strangle him, too.

Yesterday was the Christmas party at the dialysis center. No matter how I look at it, it was a lovely party, a celebration. All the patients and their families. Rockie Robinson came. Nobody had seen him since he got a cadaver transplant, and he was looking good. There is a bond between dialysis patients, like with people in AA or earthquake survivors. They are conscious of a reprieve, treat one another with more tenderness & respect than ordinary people do.

I was busy with the buffet and the punch. It was good, tons of food. No added salt. Mr. Tomanovich, Riva Chirenko's son-in-law, was a help, standing at the head of the table hailing all the guests. Food good! Drink good!

It was a lot healthier when I used to see people as animals.

Daughters

Mr. Tomanovich a sweaty manatee. Now they are all diseases. Shingles or toxic shock. Mr. Tomanovich is hypertensive, for sure, with his red face and sweaty sickles around his powder blue underarms. Potential glomerulosclerosis and renal failure. His wife, Riva Chirenko's daughter, the yak... a hysterectomy in store for her, her pain is of the womb.

Riva Chirenko herself is beyond disease. You always hear about little old ladies. The big old ladies die, that's why, except for Riva who is 280 pounds and 80 years old. Folds of red velvet spill over the plastic of her gurney. Red blood hums away. IVs drip steadily into the mesas on her arms. She looks like Father Christmas. White hair and eyebrows, rosy cheeks, white hair sprouting from her chin. She barks in Russian at her daughter, who fans her, soothes her brow with a cool cloth, sings to her in Russian in a mournful voice. Back and forth from the dining room, filling her red plate each time with morsels for her mother. Swedish meatballs, croissants with ham, roast beef, deviled eggs, asparagus, quiche, brie, olives, onion dip, pumpkin pie, champagne, cranberry juice, coffee. It all just quietly disappears into Riva Chirenko's amazingly tiny and pretty mouth.

"Where's Dr. B.?" Mr. Tomanovich keeps asking. I have worked for him for two years and I never know where he is. Is he in fact declotting a Scribner's shunt? Taking a nap? Sitting shiva? "He's in surgery," I say.

Riva Chirenko's daughter, each time she fills her mother's plate, touches Irena's, her own daughter's, hair and encourages her to eat. She says, in Russian, "Kushai, dochka." Irena's father too, comes over from time to time and says,

"Tebe nekhorosho?"

They are saying, "Shape up, you little slut!" No, of course not. They are saying, "Eat, my little princess."

The daughter, Irena, sits on the only chair in the dining room. An ugly plastic chair, all wrong. I want to throw it out, go rent her another one, buy one, quick. Her profile, with a long neck, is curved like an albino dinosaur, a marble cobra, an anorexic whippet. See, I'm sick. I make her sound grotesque. She is the most lovely creature I have ever seen. Pale green eyes, hair like white honey, like the inside of a pear. She is fourteen, in white, wearing the now-fashionable lace gloves with no fingers. Her bony hands lie in her lap like the little white birds you eat whole in Guadalajara . . . too much cinnamon. She wears white lace stockings with no feet. Pulsating blue traceries on her ankles. Her mother touches her pale hair. Irena flinches, does not acknowledge her mother at all. When her father does the same thing she doesn't speak to him, but she bares her exquisite white teeth.

Dr. B. finally arrives. There is an uproar. Patients and their families flock around him. They adore him. He looks tired. Mr. Tomanovich gets his wife to translate. He has been waiting to show Dr. B. photographs of Irena in Hawaii. Irena had won the Skagg's Drugstore Father's Day Contest. An essay: "My Dad is the Greatest!" A trip to Hawaii for her and her parents. Of course her mother couldn't leave Riva Chirenko. Irena had entered the Skagg's Mother's Day essay contest too but she had only won honorable mention and the polaroid that took all the pictures. Irena by a Bird of Paradise. Irena wearing a lei, in a sugarcane field, on the terrace. No beach. She hates the sun.

Dr. B. smiles. "You are fortunate to have such a talented and pretty child."

"God is good!" Riva Chirenko's daughter is always saying that. God brought them from Russia. God gave her mother the dialysis machine.

Dr. B. looks at Irena, sitting there, head high, scornful. Snow flakes flutter down. She raises her tiny white hand, for him to shake, kiss? It curves in the air, poised, curved. She turns into an Egyptian frieze. Dr. B. stares at her. He is transfixed.

"Have you eaten?" he asks. For God's sake. That kid hasn't eaten for years. Dr. B. goes to greet patients and guests. Irena turns her extended hand into a point toward the cloakroom. Mr. Tomanovich rushes to get her fur-trimmed coat, puts it on her. Her mother comes, buttons up the coat, frees her hair from the fur, strokes Irena's hair. Irena doesn't flinch, doesn't speak. She turns to leave. Her father touches the small of her back. She freezes and stops. He removes his hand and opens the door, following her out.

I clean up the dining room. Most of the guests have left, were leaving. The dialysis patients still have another hour on their run. Some are vomiting, some are asleep. The tape plays "Away in a manger, no crib for His bed." My own grandmother's favorite carol, but it used to scare me because she always told me not to be a dog in the manger. I thought the dog had eaten baby Jesus.

The food had been just right. Nothing is left except two large tupperware bowls that Anna Ferraza brought. A real flop. Strawberry jello & cranberries, bitter as a bog. I leave it there. The color is pretty by the red plates, the poinsettia.

There are only a few nurses and techs left. Dr. B. is on the phone in his office. The Christmas tree in the middle of the big room has hundreds of bubble lights that gurgle and flow louder than the Cobe II machines and it's as if they are transfusing the tree. You can smell the green pine of the tree. Riva Chirenko's daughter still fans Riva even though she is asleep. Finally she stops, stands. She is stiff and sore. Osteoporosis. Post-menopausal bone loss. She covers Riva with a soft shawl, comes into the dining room just as I'm leaving with a bag full of garbage. I realize that Riva Chirenko's daughter has not had dinner. She kisses my cheek. "Thank you for the party! Merry Christmas!" Her eyes are green like her daughter's. Joyous eyes. Not the sappy smile of abused children or religious fanatics. Joyous.

I empty the garbage and talk for a while with one of the techs, about saline, where to get his wife a sweater. I check with the answering service to see if there are any messages. Hyper-al orders for Ruttle, that's it. Maisie, the operator, asks if I have tomorrow off. Yes! God is good, Maisie. She laughs. Not to me, he ain't.

I go get my coat. I remember the cranberry jello, realize that Riva Chirenko's daughter will eat it, enjoy it.

Bluebonnets

"Ma, I can't believe you are doing this. You never even go out with anybody, and here you are spending a week with some stranger. He could be an ax-murderer for all you know."

Maria's son Nick was taking her to the Oakland airport. Lord, why hadn't she taken a cab? Her sons, all grown now, could be worse than parents, more judgemental, more old-fashioned when it came to her.

"I haven't met him, but he's not exactly a stranger. He liked my poetry, asked me to translate his book to Spanish. We have written and spoken on the phone for years. We have a lot in common. He raised his four sons alone, too. I garden; he has a farm. I'm flattered that he invited me . . . I don't think he sees many people."

Maria had asked an old friend in Austin about Dixon. A genius. Total eccentric, Ingeborg had said. Never socializes. Instead of a briefcase he has a gunny sack. His students either idolize him or hate him. He's in his late forties, quite attractive. Let me know everything . . .

"That was the weirdest book I ever read," Nick said, "not that I could read it. Admit it . . . could you? Enjoy it, I mean."

"The language was great. Clear and simple. Nice to translate. It is philosophy and linguistics, just very abstract."

"I can't imagine you doing this . . . having some kind of a fling . . . in Texas."

So Long: Stories

"That's what's bothering you. The idea that your mother might have sex, or that somebody in her fifties might. Anyway he didn't say 'Let's have a fling.' He said, 'Why not come to my farm for a week? The bluebonnets have just begun to bloom. I can show you notes for my new book. We can fish, go for walks in the woods.' Give me a break, Nick. I work in a county hospital, in Oakland. How do you think a walk in the woods sounds to me? Bluebonnets? I may as well be going to heaven."

They pulled up in front of United and Nick got her bag from the trunk. He hugged her, kissed her cheek. "Sorry I gave you a hard time. Enjoy your trip, Ma. Hey, maybe you can get to a Rangers' game."

Snow on the Rocky Mountains. Marie read, listened to music, tried not to think. Of course, in the back of her mind, there was the idea of an affair.

She hadn't taken off her clothes since she had stopped drinking, the idea was terrifying. Well, he sounded pretty stuffy himself, maybe he felt the same way. Take it a day at a time. Practice just being with a man, for lord's sake, enjoy the visit. You're going to Texas.

The parking lot smelled like Texas. *Caliche* dust and oleander. He tossed her bag into the bed of an old Dodge pickup truck with dog scratches on the doors. "You know 'Tennessee Border'?" Maria asked. "Sure do." They sang it. ". . . Picked her up in a pickup truck and she broke that heart of mine." Dixon was tall, lean, good laugh lines. Squint lines around open grey eyes. He was entirely at ease, asked her one personal question after another in a nasal drawl just like her Uncle John's. How did she know Texas, that old song? Why did she get divorced? What were her sons like? Why didn't she drink? Why was she an alcoholic? Why did she translate other people's work? The questions were embarrassing, buffeting, but soothing, the attention, like a massage.

He stopped at a fish market. Stay here, be right back. Then the freeway and hot gusts of air. Down onto a ribbon of macadam road where they never saw another car. One slow red tractor. Windmills, Hereford cattle knee deep in Indian paintbrush. In the small town of Brewster, Dixon parked across from the town square. Haircut. She followed him past the barber's pole into a one-chair barber shop, sat listening while he and the old man cutting his hair discussed the heat, the rains, fishing, Jesse Jackson running for president, several deaths and a marriage. Dixon had just grinned at her when she asked if her bag would be all right in the back of the truck. She looked out the window at downtown Brewster. It was early afternoon and no one was walking in the streets. Two old men sat on the courthouse steps like extras in a southern movie, chewing tobacco, spitting.

The absence of noise was what was so evocative of her childhood, of another era. No sirens, no traffic, no radios. A horsefly buzzed against the window, snip of scissors, the rhythm of the two men's voices, an electric fan with dirty ribbons flying rustled old magazines. The barber ignored her, not out of rudeness but from courtesy.

Dixon said "much obliged" when he left. As they walked across the square to the grocery store she told him about her Texan grandma Mamie. Once an old woman had stopped by to visit. Mamie had served tea in a pot with a sugar bowl and creamer, little sandwiches, cookies and cut-up pieces of cake. "Mercy, Mamie, you shouldn't go to so much trouble." "Oh, yes," Mamie had said, "one always should."

They put the groceries in the back of the truck and drove to the feed store, where Dixon got mash and chicken feed, two bales of hay, a dozen baby chicks. He smiled at her when he caught her staring at him and two farmers talking about alfalfa.

"What would you be doing now, in Oakland?" he asked when they got in the truck. Today was pediatric clinic. Crack babies, gun-shot wounds, AIDS babies. Hernias and tumors, but mostly wounds of the city's desperate and angry poor.

They were soon out of the town and on a narrow dirt road. The baby chicks chirped in the box on the floor.

"This is what I wanted you to see," he said, "the road to my place this time of year."

They drove along the empty road over gently rolling hills, fragrant and lush with flowers, pink, blue, magenta, red. Bursts of yellow and lavender. The hot, perfumed air enveloped the cab. Huge thunderclouds had formed and the light grew yellow, giving miles of flowers an iridescent luminosity. Larks and meadowlarks, redwinged blackbirds darted above the ditches by the road; the singing of the birds rose above the sound of the truck. Maria leaned out of the window, her damp head resting on her arms. It was only April, but the heavy Texan heat suffused her, the perfume of the flowers lulled like a drug.

An old tin-roofed farm house with a rocking chair on the porch, a dozen or so kittens of different ages. They put the groceries away in a kitchen with fine Sarouk rugs in front of the sink and stove, another burnt by sparks from a wood stove. Two leather chairs. Bookcases lined the walls, with books two-deep. A massive oak table covered with books. Columns of books were stacked on the floor. The old, rippled glass windows looked out onto a field of rich green pasture where kid goats suckled their mothers. Dixon put the food into the refrigerator, put the chicks in a larger box on the floor, with a light bulb in it, even though it was so warm. His dog had just died, he said. And then for the first time seemed self-conscious. Need to water, he said, and she followed him past the chicken sheds and barns to a large field planted with corn, tomatoes, beans, squash and other vegetables. She sat on the fence while he opened sluice gates to start the water into the furrows. A chestnut mare and colt galloped in the field of bluebonnets beyond.

It was late afternoon when they fed the animals by the barn, where in a dark comer dripped cloth bags filled with cheese, and more cats scampered along the rafters, indifferent to the birds that flitted in and out of the upper windows by the lofts. An old white mule, Homer, lumbered up when he heard the sound of the bucket. Lie down with me, Dixon said. But they'll step on us. No, just lie down. A circle of goats blocked out the sun, their long-lashed eyes gazing down at her. Nuzzle of Homer's velvety lips on Maria's cheeks. The mare and the colt snorted, spraying hot breaths as they checked her out.

The other rooms in the farm house were not like the cluttered kitchen at all. One room with wooden plank floors, nothing in it but a Steinway grand. Dixon's study, which was bare except for four large wooden tables covered with 5" by 8" white cards. Each one of them had a paragraph or a sentence on them. She saw that he shuffled them around, the way other people move things in a computer. Don't look at those now, he said.

His living room and bedroom were one large room with tall windows on two sides. Large lush paintings on the other two walls. Maria was surprised that they were done by Dixon. He was so quiet. The paintings were bold, lavish. He had painted a mural on his corduroy couch, figures, sitting there. A brass bed with an old patchwork quilt, exquisite chests and desks and tables, early American antiques that had belonged to his father. The floor in this room was painted glossy white under more priceless Persian rugs. Be sure and take off your shoes, he said.

Her room was a sun porch along the back of the house, with screens on three sides of a meshed plastic that blurred the pink and green flowers, the new green of the trees, the flash of a cardinal. It was like the basement of L'Orangerie where you sit surrounded by Monet's water-lilies. He was filling the bath-tub for her in the next room. You'll probably want to lie down awhile. I've got some more chores to do.

Clean, tired, she lay surrounded by the soft colors that blurred when the rain began and the wind swirled the leaves in the trees. Rain on a tin roof. Just as she fell asleep Dixon came and lay down beside her, lay next to her until she woke and they made love, simple as that.

Dixon built a fire in the iron stove and she sat by it while he made crab gumbo. He cooked on a hot plate but had a dishwasher. They ate on the porch by lantern light while the rain abated and when the clouds cleared turned off the lantern to look at the stars.

They fed the animals at the same time each day but the rest of the days and nights got turned around. They stayed in bed all day, had breakfast when it got dark, walked in the woods by the light of the moon. They watched *Mr. Lucky* with Cary Grant at three in the morning. Lazy in the hot sun they rocked in the rowboat on the pond, fishing, reading John Donne, William Blake. They lay in the damp grass, watching the chickens, talking about their childhoods, their children. They watched Nolan Ryan shut out the A's, slept in sleeping bags by a lake hours away through the brush. They made love in the claw-foot tub, in the rowboat, in the woods, but mostly in the shimmering green of the sun porch when it rained.

What was love? Maria asked herself, watching the clean lines of his face as he slept. What's to keep the two of us from doing it, loving.

They both admitted how rarely they spoke with anyone, laughed at themselves for how much they had to say now, how they interrupted each other, yes, but. It was hard when he talked about his new book or referred to Heidegger and Wittgenstein, Derrida, Chomsky and others whose names she didn't even recognize.

"I'm sorry. I'm a poet. I deal with the specific. I am lost with the abstract. I simply don't have the background to discuss this with you."

Dixon was furious. "How the devil did you translate my other book? I know you did a good job by the response it got. Did you read the damn thing?"

Bluebonnets

"I did do a good job. I didn't distort a word. Someone could translate my poems perfectly but still think they were personal and trivial. I didn't...grasp...the philosophical implications in the book."

"Then this visit is a farce. My books are everything I am. It is pointless for us to discuss anything at all."

Maria started to feel hurt and angry and to let him go out the door alone. But she followed him, sat down beside him on the porch step. "It's not pointless. And I'm learning about who you are." Dixon held her then, kissed her, gingerly.

While he had been a student he had lived in a cabin a few acres away, in the woods. An old man had lived in this house and Dixon had done errands for him, brought him food and supplies from town. When the old man died he left the house and ten acres to Dixon, the rest of his land to the state for a bird sanctuary. They hiked the next morning to his old cabin. He had even had to carry in his water, he said. It was the best period of his life.

The wooden cabin was in a grove of cottonwood. There had been no path to it, and there seemed to be no landmarks at all in the scrub oak and mesquite. As they got close to it Dixon cried out, as if in pain.

Someone, kids probably, had shot out all the windows of the cabin, hacked up the inside with axes, spray-painted obscenities on the bare pine walls. It was hard to imagine anyone coming so far into the wilderness to do this. It looks like Oakland, Maria said. Dixon glared at her, turned around and started walking back through the trees. She kept him in sight but could not keep up with him. It was eerily quiet. Every once in a while there would be an enormous Brahma bull in the shade of a tree. Just standing there, unblinking, stolid, silent.

Dixon didn't speak on the drive home. Green grasshoppers clicked against the windshield. "I'm sorry, about what happened to your house," she said and when he didn't answer she said,

"I do that too, when I feel pain. Crawl under the house like a sick cat." He still said nothing. When they pulled up outside his house he reached over and opened her door. The engine was still running. "I'm going to go get my mail. Back in a while. Maybe you could read some of my book."

She knew that by book he meant the hundreds of cards on the tables. Why had he asked her to do that now? Maybe it was because he couldn't talk. She did that sometimes. When she wanted to tell someone how she felt it was too hard so she would show them a poem. Usually they didn't understand what she had intended.

With a sick feeling she went into the house. It would be fine to live where you didn't even close your doors. She started into Dixon's living room to put on some music, but changed her mind, went into the room with the cards. She sat on a stool that she moved from table to table as she read and re-read the sentences on the cards.

"You have no idea what they say, do you?" He had come in silently, was standing behind her as she leaned over the table. She had not touched any of the cards.

He began to move them around the table, frantically, like someone playing that game where you line up numbers correctly. Maria left and went out on the porch.

"I asked you not to walk on that floor with shoes on."

"What floor? What are you talking about?"

"The white floor."

"I haven't been near that room. You are crazy."

"Don't lie to me. They are your footprints."

"Oh, Sorry. I did start to go in there. I couldn't have taken more than two steps."

"Exactly. Two."

"Thank God I'm going home in the morning. I'm going for a walk right now."

84

Bluebonnets

Maria walked down the path toward the pond, got into the green rowboat and shoved herself away from the bank. She laughed at herself when the dragonflies reminded her of Oakland police helicopters.

Dixon strode down the path to the pond, walked out into the water and pulled himself into the boat. He kissed her, pinned her down into the watery bed of the boat while he entered her. They clashed wildly into each other and the boat bobbed and spun until it finally moored itself in the reeds. They lay there, rocking in the hot sun. She wondered if so much passion had come from simple rage or from a sense of loss. They made love wordlessly most of the night, in the sun porch to the sound of the rain. Before the rain they had heard the cry of a coyote, the squawk of the chickens as they roosted in the trees.

They rode to the airport in silence, past the miles of bluebonnets and primrose. Just drop me off, she said, not that much time.

Maria took a cab home from the airport to her high-rise apartment in Oakland. Hello to the security guard, check the mail. The elevator was empty, as were the halls during the day. She put down her suitcase inside her door and turned on the air. She took off her shoes, as everyone did when they walked on her carpet. She went into the bedroom and lay down on her own bed.

La Vie en Rose

The two girls lie face down upon towels that say Grand Hotel Pucón. The sand is black and fine; the water in the lake is green. Deeper sweet green the pines that edge the lake. Villarica volcano towers white above the lake and the trees, the hotel, the village of Pucón. Spumes of smoke rise from the volcano's cone and vanish into the clear blue of the sky. Blue beach cabañas. Gerda's cap of red hair, a yellow beach ball, the red sashes of *huasos* cantering among the trees.

Once in a while one of Gerda's or Claire's tan legs waves languidly in the air, shaking off sand, a fly. Sometimes their young bodies quiver with the helpless giggle of adolescent girls.

"And the look on Conchi's face! All she could think of it say was '*Ojalá.*' What nerve!"

Gerda's laugh is a short germanic bark. Claire's is high, rippling.

"She won't admit how silly she was either."

Claire sits up to put oil on her face. Her blue eyes scan the beach. Nada. The two handsome men haven't reappeared.

"There she is . . . the Anna Karenina woman . . ."

On a red and white canvas chair beneath the pines. The melancholy Russian lady in a panama hat, with a white silk parasol.

Gerda groans. "Oh, she's lovely. Her nose. Grey flannel in summer. And she looks so miserable. She must have a lover."

"I'm going to cut my hair like hers."

"On you it would look like you put a bowl on your head. She just has style."

"She's the only one here who does. All these tacky Argentines and Americans. There don't seem to be any Chileans at all, not even on the staff. The whole village was speaking German."

"When I wake up I think at first that I'm a little girl in Germany or Switzerland. I can hear the maids whispering in the hall, singing from the kitchen."

"Nobody's smiling but those Americans, not even those children, so serious with their pails."

"Only Americans smile all the time. You're speaking in Spanish but your silly grin gives you away. Your father laughs all the time too. The bottom just dropped out of the copper market, haha."

"Your father laughs a lot too."

"Only when something is stupid. Look at him. He must have swum to that raft a hundred times this morning."

Gerda and Claire always go places with one of their fathers. To movies and horse races with Mr. Thompson, to the symphony or to play golf with Herr Von Dessaur. In contrast, their Chilean friends are invariably with mothers and aunts, grandmothers and sisters.

Gerda's mother was killed in Germany during the war; her stepmother is a physician, rarely at home. Claire's mother drinks, is in bed or sanatoriums most of the time. After school the two friends go home to tea, to read or study. Their friendship began over books, in their empty houses.

Herr von Dessaur dries himself. He is wet, out of breath. Cool grey eyes. As a child Claire had felt guilty watching war movies. She liked the Nazis . . . their overcoats, their cars, cool grey eyes.

"Ja. Enough. Go swim. Let me see your crawls, how you are diving now."

"He's being nice, no?" Claire says on the way to the water.

"He's nice when he is not with her."

La Vie en Rose

The girls swim with sure strokes far out into the icy lake, until they hear *Gerdalein!* and see her father waving. They swim to the raft, lie warm against the wood. The white volcano sparkles and smokes high above them. Laughter from a boat far out on the lake, hoof-beats on the dirt road by the shore. No other sound. Lap, lap of the water against the rocking raft.

In the vast high-ceilinged dining room white curtains billow in the breeze from the lake. Palm leaves fan in urns. One waiter in tails ladles the consommé, another breaks eggs, drops one into each pewter bowl. Together the two men bone trout, ignite desserts.

A stooped white-haired gentleman sits down across from the beautiful Anna Karenina.

"Could he be her husband?"

"I hope he isn't Count Vronsky."

"Where did you girls get the idea that they were Russians? I heard them speaking German."

"Really, Papi? What did they say?"

"She said, 'I shouldn't have eaten prunes for breakfast.'"

The girls rent a rowboat, set out for an island. The lake is immense. They take turns, laughing, paddling in circles at first but then gliding smooth. Splash and dip of the oars. They beach the boat in a cove, dive from a rock ledge into the green water that tastes of fish and moss. They swim for a long time and then lie spread-eagled in the sun, their faces buried in wild clover. There is a long slow tremor that rolls and shudders the ground beneath their young bodies. They cling to the clumps of lavender blossoms as the earth undulates below them, away from under them. Their eyes are level with the green rippling of the land. Does it grow dark with smoke from the volcano? The odor of sulphur is intense, terrifying. The temblor stops. For a split second there is no sound and then the birds burst into an alarm of hysterical chatter. Cows low and horses whinny from all around the lake. Dogs are barking, barking. Above the girls the birds whirr and whistle in the branches of the trees. High waves slap against the stones. The girls are silent. Neither can speak about what she feels, something different from fear. Gerda laughs, her bark of a laugh.

« · »

"We swam for miles, Papi. Look at our hands, blisters from rowing! Did you feel the tremor?"

He had been playing golf when the temblor came, was on the green. A golfer's nightmare . . . to see your ball coming away from the hole, toward you!

The young men are in the lobby, talking with the desk clerk. Oh, they are handsome. Strong and tanned with white teeth. They are flashily dressed, in their mid-twenties. Claire's, the dark one, has a cleft chin. When he looks down his lashes brush high bronzed cheekbones. Be still, my heart! Claire laughs. Herr von Dessaur says the men are far too old, and vulgar, clearly the worst sort. Farmers, probably. He escorts the girls past them, instructs them to read in their room until dinner.

The dining room is festive. Because of the temblor people nod to the other patrons, speak to the waiters, chat with each other. There are musicians, very old men. Violins play tangos, waltzes. *Frenesi. La Mer.*

The young men stand in the doorway, framed by potted palms and sconces of wine-colored velvet.

"Papi, they're not farmers. Look!"

They are resplendent in powder blue uniforms of Chilean aviation cadets. Pale blue trimmed with gold braid. High collars and epaulets, gold buttons. They wear boots with spurs, floor length woolen capes, swords. They hold their hats and gloves in the crooks of their arms.

"Military! Worse!" Herr von Dessaur laughs. He averts his face, wiping tears of laughter from his eyes.

La Vie en Rose

"Capes on a summer night. Spurs and swords in an airplane? For God's sake, just look at the poor fools!"

Claire and Gerda stare at them with awe. The cadets return their looks with soulful gazes, half-smiles. They sit at a little table by the bandstand, drinking brandy from huge snifters. The blond one has a tortoise-shell cigarette holder which he clamps between his teeth.

"Papi, admit it. His eyes are the very same blue as his cape."

"Yes. Chilean Air Force Blue. The Chilean Air Force does not even have any airplanes!"

It must have been too hot after all. They move to a table by the door to the terrace, drape their capes on their chairs.

The girls plead to be able to stay up longer, to listen to the music, watch the people tango. Sweat curls the hair on the brows of the dancers whose eyes are locked, hypnotized. Sleepwalking, the dancers twirl and dip to the violins.

The men, Roberto and Andrés, click the heels of their boots. They introduce themselves to Gerda's father, ask for his kind permission to dance with the two young ladies. Herr von Dessaur starts to refuse but still finds the cadets so amusing he says one dance and then it's time for the girls to go to bed.

La Vie en Rose the orchestra plays for a very long time as the young people dance around and around on the polished floor. The blue uniforms, the white chiffon dresses reflect in the dark mirrors. People smile, watching the beautiful dancers. Curtains billow like sails. Andrés speaks to Claire in the familiar tense. Roberto suggests that the girls come back downstairs after Herr von Dessaur goes to sleep. The dance is over.

Days go by. The men work on Roberto's fundo, come to the hotel only in the evening. Gerda and Claire swim, climb the volcano. Hot sun, cool snow. They play golf and croquet with Herr von Dessaur. They row to their island. They ride horseback with Herr von Dessaur. Shoulders back he says. Head up he says to Claire. He holds her throat for a long time. Claire swallows.

So Long: Stories

The girls play canasta with some ladies on the terrace. An Argentine woman reads their fortunes with cards. A cigarette in her mouth; she squints through the smoke. Gerda gets a new path and a strange, mysterious man. Claire gets a new path too and the 2 of hearts. A kiss from the gods.

Every night they dance with Roberto and Andrés to *La Vie en Rose* and finally one night the girls do go back downstairs after Herr von Dessaur is asleep. A honeymoon couple and some Americans are the only people left in the dining room. Roberto & Andrés stand and bow. The old men in the orchestra look shocked but they play *Adiós Muchachos*, a mournful, pulsating tango. The couples dance dreamily out the doors to the terrace, down the steps to the wet sand. Boots crunch on the sand like on new snow. They climb into a boat. They sit in the starlit night, holding hands, listening to the violins. The lights from the hotel and the white volcano splinter silver in the water. A breeze. It is cool. No, it is cold. The boat has come unmoored. There are no oars. The boat is moving fast, gliding like the wind, with the wind, out into the dark lake. Oh, no! Gerda gasps. The girls are kissed while there is still a chance. He put his whole tongue in my mouth, Gerda says, later. Claire is bumped on the forehead. A kiss catches the corner of her lips, grazes her nose before the girls dive like mercury into the black water of the lake.

Their shoes are gone. The girls are wet and cold, shivering outside the doorway to the hotel, shuttered now by iron gates. Let's just wait, Claire says. What, until morning? You must be mad! Gerda shakes the metal gates until at last lights go on in the hotel. Gerdalein! her father says from a balcony, but suddenly he is in front of them, behind the gates. The mayordomo is in a bathrobe, with keys.

In their room the girls wrap themselves in blankets. Herr von Dessaur is pale. Did he touch you? Gerda shakes her head. No. We danced and then we sat in a boat but then the boat got loose so we ... Did he kiss you? She doesn't answer. I ask you.

Did he kiss you? Gerda nods her head; her father slaps her in the mouth. Slut, he says.

The maid comes in the morning before it is light. She packs their bags. They leave before anyone is awake, wait a long time at the railway station in Temuco. Herr von Dessaur sits across from Claire and Gerda. The girls are reading, silently, the book held between them. *Sonata de Otoño*. The woman dies in his arms, in a distant wing of the castle. He has to carry her body back to her own bed, through the passages. Her long black hair catches on the stones. No candle.

"You will see no one, and especially not Claire, for the rest of the summer."

Finally Herr von Dessaur goes out to smoke and for just a short blessed time the friends can laugh. A joyous splutter of laughter. By the time he returns they are reading quietly.

Macadam

When fresh it looks like caviar, sounds like broken glass, like someone chewing ice.

I'd chew ice when the lemonade was finished, swaying with my grandmother on the porch swing. We gazed down upon the chain-gang paving Upson Street. A foreman poured the macadam; the convicts stomped it down with a heavy rhythmic beat. The chains rang; the macadam made the sound of applause.

The three of us said the word often. My mother because she hated where we lived, in squalor, and at least now we would have a macadam street. My grandmother just so wanted things clean – it would hold down the dust. Red Texan dust that blew in with gray tailings from the smelter, sifting into dunes on the polished hall floor, onto her mahogany table.

I used to say macadam out loud, to myself, because it sounded like the name for a friend.

Love Affair

Dear Conchi,

...The University of New Mexico, not how we imagined it
at all. Secondary school in Chile was harder than college here.
I live in a dorm, hundreds of girls, all outgoing and confident.
I still feel strange, ill at ease.

I love the place itself. The campus has many old adobe buildings. The desert is beautiful and there are mountains here. Not
like the Andes of course, but big on a different scale. Rugged
and rocky. Dumb-dumb...that's what they are called, the Rocky
Mountains. Clear clean air, cold at night with millions of stars.

My clothes are all wrong. A girl even told me that nobody
here "dresses up" like I do. I have to get white sox I guess and
huge circular skirts, blue jeans. I mean, the women look really
horrible. It's nice on the men, though, casual clothes and boots.

I'll never get used to the food. Cereal for breakfast and coffee
as weak as tea. And when I'm ready for tea in the afternoon
that's when dinner is served here. When I'm ready for dinner
it's lights-out time at the dorm.

I couldn't get a class with Ramon Sender until next semester.
I saw him in the hall, though! I told him *Cronica del Alba* was
my favorite book. He said, "Yes, but then, you are very young."
He is how I imagined him, only real old. Very Spanish and arrogant, dignified...

So Long: Stories

《 · 》

Dear Conchi,

I have a job, can you imagine? Part time, but still. It's proof-reading the college paper, *The Lobo*, that comes out once a week. I work three nights in the journalism building, right next to the dorm. I even have a key to the dorm, since it's locked at ten and I work until eleven. The printer is an old Texan called Jonesy, who works on a linotype machine. A wonderful machine with about a thousand parts and gears. Boiling lead that makes the letters. He puts the words in and they clank and sing and clatter, come out in lines of hot lead. It makes each line seem important.

He teaches me things, about writing headlines, which stories are good, and why. He teases me a lot, plays tricks to keep me on my toes. In the middle of a story about a basketball game he'll slip in something like "Down upon the Swanee River."

Sometimes a man called Joe Sanchez comes in and brings copy and a beer for Jonesy. He's a sports and feature writer. He's a student, but much older than the boys in my classes, because he is a veteran, here on the GI bill. He tells us about Japan, where he was a medic. He looks like an Indian, has shiny black hair, long, combed in a duck-tail.

Sorry, I'm already using expressions you've never heard. Most of the boys here wear crew cuts, which is practically shaven heads. Some have longer hair, combed back in what looks like a duck's tail.

I miss you and Quena a lot. I haven't made a friend yet. I am different, coming from Chile. I think people think I'm stuck up because I'm not open. I don't understand the humor yet, get embarrassed because there's a lot of joking and hinting about sex. Strangers will tell you their whole life story, but they aren't emotional or affectionate like Chileans, so I still don't feel I know them.

Love Affair

All those years in South America I wanted to return to my country the U.S.A. because it was a democracy, not with just two classes like Chile. There are definitely classes here. Girls who were nice to me in the beginning snub me now because I didn't go through rush, live in the dorm and not a sorority. And some sororities are "better" than others. Richer.

I mentioned to my roommate Ella that Joe, the reporter, was funny and nice and she said "Yes, but he's Mexican." He's not from Mexico, that's what they call anybody of Spanish descent here. There aren't that many Mexicans at the university, when you consider the population here, and only about ten Negroes.

My journalism classes are going well, great teachers, they even look like reporters in old movies. I'm starting to get a weird feeling though. I majored in journalism because I wanted to be a writer, but the whole point of journalism is to cut out all the good stuff...

« · »

Dear Conchi,

...I have been out several times with Joe Sanchez. He gets free tickets to events so he'll do stories on them. I like him because he never says things just because they are the right thing to say. It's very cool to like Dave Brubeck, a jazz musician, but in his review Joe called him a wimp. People got really mad. And Billy Graham. Hard to explain to you, being Catholic, what an Evangelist is. He talks, hollers, about God and sin and tries to get people to turn their lives over to Jesus. Everybody I know thinks the guy is crazy, money hungry and hopelessly corny. The column Joe wrote was about the man's skill and power. It turned into a column about faith.

We don't go to student hang-outs afterwards but to little restaurants in the South Valley or to Mexican bars or cowboy bars. It's like being in another country. We drive up into the mountains or out into the desert, walk or climb for miles. He doesn't try to "make out" (*atracar*) like all the other boys do, relentlessly, here. When he says goodbye he just touches my cheek. Once he kissed my hair.

He doesn't talk about things, or events or books. He reminds me of my uncle John. He tells stories, about his brothers, or his grandfather, or geisha girls in Japan.

I like him because he talks to everybody. He really wants to know what everyone is up to.

« · »

Dear Conchi,

I'm going out with a really sophisticated man, Bob Dash. We went to a play, *Waiting for Godot*, and to an Italian movie, I forget the title. He looks like a handsome author on a book jacket. A pipe, patches on his elbows. He lives in an adobe house filled with Indian pots and rugs and modern art. We drink gin and tonics with lime in them, listen to music like Bartok's "Sonata for two pianos and percussion." He talks a lot about books I have never heard of, and has lent me a dozen books . . . Sartre, Keerke-gard (sp?), Becket and T. S. Eliot, many more. I like a poem called "The Hollow Men."

Joe told me it was Dash who was a hollow man. He has been unreasonably upset about me going out with Bob, or even having coffee with him. He says he's not jealous but that he can't bear the idea of me becoming an intellectual. Says I have to listen to Patsy Cline and Charlie Parker as an antidote. Read Walt Whitman and Thomas Wolfe's *Look Homeward, Angel*.

Actually I liked Camus' *The Stranger* better than *Look Home-ward, Angel*. But I like Joe because he likes that book. He's not afraid to be corny. He loves America, and New Mexico, the *barrio* where he lives, the desert. We go for long hikes in the foothills. Once a huge duststorm came up. Tumbleweeds

Love Affair

whipping through the air and blizzards of yellow dust howling. He was dancing around in it. I could barely hear him hollering how wonderful it was, the desert. We saw a coyote, heard it yelping.

He's corny with me, too. He remembers things, and listens to me go on and on. Once I was crying for no reason, just missing you and Quena and home. He didn't try to cheer me up, just held me and let me be sad. We speak Spanish when we're talking about sweet things, or when we're kissing. We've been kissing a lot.

《 · 》

Dear Conchi,

I wrote a short story, "Apples." It's about an old man who rakes apples. Bob Dash red-penciled about a dozen adjectives and said it was "an acceptable little story." Joe said it was precious and false. That I should only write about what I feel, not make up something about an old man I never knew. It doesn't bother me what they said. I read it over and over.

Of course it bothers me.

Ella, my roommate, said she would prefer not to read it. I wish we got along better. Her mother mails her her Kotex from Oklahoma every month. She's a drama major. God, how can she ever play Lady Macbeth if she can't relax about a little blood?

I'm seeing more of Bob Dash. He's like having a personal seminar. Today we went to coffee and talked about *Nausea*. But I'm thinking more about Joe. I see him between classes and when I'm working. He and Jonesy and I laugh a lot, eat pizza and drink beer. Joe has a little room that's sort of his office, that's where we kiss. I don't think about him exactly, but about kissing him. I was thinking about it in Copy Editing 1, and even groaned or said something out loud and the professor looked at me and said "Yes, Miss Gray?"

So Long: Stories

« · »

Dear Conchi,

... I'm reading Jane Austen. Her writing is like chamber music, but it's real and funny at the same time. There are a thousand books I want to read, don't know where to start. I'm changing my major to English next semester...

« · »

Dear Conchi,

An old couple work as janitors in the journalism building. One night they took us up on the roof for a beer after work. The roof is overhung with cottonwood trees and you can just sit under the trees and look at the stars. If you want you can look over and watch the cars on Route 66, or on the other side, into the windows of the dorm where I live. They gave us an extra key to the broom closet, where the ladder to the roof is. Nobody else knows about this place. We go up there between classes and after work. Joe brought a grill and a mattress and candles. It's like our own island or tree house...

« · »

Dear Conchi,

I am happy. When I wake up in the morning my face is sore from smiling.

When I was little I think I felt peace sometimes, in the woods or a meadow, and in Chile I was always having fun. I felt joy when I skied. But I had never felt happiness like I do with Joe. Never felt that I was me, and loved for that.

I sign out for the weekends to his house, with his father responsible for me. Joe lives with his father, who is very old, a retired school teacher. He loves to cook, makes awful greasy

Love Affair

food. He drinks beer all day. The only effect it seems to have is to make him sing things like "Minnie the Mermaid" and "Rain on the Roof," over and over while he cooks. He tells stories too, about everybody in Armijo, the neighborhood. He had most of them in school.

《 · 》

Dear Conchi,

Most weekends we go to the Jemez mountains and climb all day, camp out at night. There are some hot springs up there. So far nobody has been there when we have. Deer and owls, big-horned sheep, blue jays. We lie in the water, talk or read out loud. Joe loves to read Keats.

My classes and job are going fine, but I always can't wait until they are over so I can be with Joe. He's a sports reporter for the *Tribune*, too, so it's hard to find time. We go to track meets and high school basketball games, stock car races. I don't like football, miss soccer and rugby games.

《 · 》

Dear Conchi,

Everyone is unreasonably upset about me and Joe. The house-mother gave me a talk. Bob Dash was horrid, lectured me for about an hour, until I got up and left. Said Joe was vulgar and common, a hedonist with no sense of values and no intellectual scope. Among other things. Mostly people are worried because I'm so young. They think I'm going to throw away my education or career. Or that's what they all say. I think they are jealous because we are so in love. And no matter what their arguments, from ruining my reputation to risking my future, they always bring up the fact that he is Mexican. It never occurs to anybody that coming from Chile I would naturally like a latin person, someone who feels things. I don't fit in here at all. I wish Joe and I could go home to Santiago . . .

«·»

Dear Conchi,

. . . Someone actually wrote to my parents, told them I was having an affair with a man much too old for me. They called, hysterical, are coming all the way from Chile. They will arrive on New Year's Eve. Apparently my mother started drinking again. My father says it's all my fault.

When I'm with Joe none of this matters. I think he is a reporter because he likes to talk to people. Wherever we go we end up talking to strangers. And liking them.

I don't think I ever really liked the world until I met him. My parents don't like the world, or me, or they would trust me.

«·»

Dear Conchi,

They arrived on New Year's Eve, but were exhausted from the trip so we only talked for a little while. They didn't hear that I'm making straight A's, that I love my job, that I was chosen queen of the Newsprint Ball that night. I have become a fallen woman, a common tart, etc. "With a greaser," my mother said.

The dance was wonderful. We had dinner with friends from the department before the dance, laughed a lot. There was a ceremony where I got a newspaper crown and an orchid. For some reason I had never danced with Joe before. It was wonderful. Dancing with him.

We had agreed to see my parents the next day, at their motel. My father said he and Joe could watch the Rose Bowl game, that it would break the ice.

I am so dumb. I saw that they had been drinking martinis

already, felt they would be more relaxed. Joe was great. At ease, warm, open. They were like stone.

Daddy relaxed a little when the game came on, both he and Joe enjoyed it. Mama and I sat there silent. Joe just drinks beer, so he really loosened up on my father's martinis. Every time there was a field goal he'd holler "Fuckin' A!" or "*A la verga!*" A few times he punched Daddy on the shoulder. Mama cringed and drank and didn't say a word.

After the game Joe invited my parents out to dinner, but my father said that he and Joe should go get some Chinese food.

While they were gone Mama talked about the shame I had caused them by being immoral, how disgusted she was.

Conchi, I know we promised to tell the other about sex, the first time either of us made love. It's hard to write about. What is fine about it is that it is between two people, the most naked and close you can get. And each time is different and a surprise. Sometimes we laugh the whole time. Sometimes it makes you cry.

Sex is the most important thing that ever happened to me. I could not understand what my mother was saying, that I was filthy.

Lord knows what Joe and Daddy talked about. They were both pale when they got back. Apparently my father said things like "statutory rape" and Joe said he would marry me tomorrow, which was the worst thing, for my parents, that he could have said.

After we had eaten Joe said, "Well, we're all pretty tired. I better be going. You coming, Lu?"

"No, She's staying here," my father said.

I stood there, frozen.

"I'm going with Joe," I said. "I'll see you in the morning."

I'm writing you now from the dorm. It's eerily quiet. Most of the girls went home for Christmas.

Except for briefly telling me what my father said, Joe didn't talk while he drove me home. I couldn't talk either. When we kissed goodbye I thought my heart would break.

《 · 》

Dear Conchi,

My parents are taking me out of school at the end of the semester. They'll wait for me in New York. I'm to go there and then we're going to Europe until the fall semester.

I took a taxi to Joe's house. We were going to Sandia Peak to talk, got into the car. I don't know what I thought he would say, what I wanted.

I hoped he'd say he'd wait for me, that he'd still be here when I got back. But he said that if I really loved him I'd marry him right now. I reacted to that. He needs to graduate; he only works part-time. I didn't say more of the truth which is that I don't want to leave school. I want to study Shakespeare, the Romantic poets. He said we could live with his dad until we had enough money. We were crossing the bridge over the Rio Grande when I said I didn't want to get married yet.

"You won't know for a long time what it is you're throwing away."

I said I knew what we had, that it would still be there when I got back.

"It will, but you won't. No, you'll go on, have 'relationships,' marry some asshole."

He opened the car door, shoved me out onto the Rio Grande bridge, the car still moving. He drove away. I walked all the way across town to the dorm. I kept thinking he'd pull up behind me, but he never did.

Our Brother's Keeper

When some people die they just vanish, like pebbles into a pool. Everyday life just smooths back together and goes on as it did before. Other people die but stay around for a long time, either because they have captured the public's imagination, like James Dean, or because their spirit just won't let go, like our friend Sara's.

Sara died ten years ago, but still, anytime her grandchildren say something bright or imperious, everyone will say, "She's just like Sara!" Whenever I see two women driving along and laughing together, really laughing, I always think it's Sara. And of course each spring when I plant I remember the fig tree we got in the garbage bin at PayLess, the bad fight we had over the miniature coral rose bush at East Bay.

Our country has just gone to war, which is why I'm thinking about her now. She could get madder at our politicians, and be more vocal about it, than anybody I know. I want to call her up; she always gave you something to do, made you feel you could do something.

Even though all of us continue to reminisce about her, we stopped talking about the way she died very soon after it happened. She was murdered, brutally, her head bashed in with a "blunt instrument." A lover she had been going with had repeatedly threatened to kill her. She had called the police each time but they said there was nothing they could do. The man was a dentist, an alcoholic, some fifteen years younger than she was. In spite of the threats, and of other times that he had hit her, no weapon was found, no evidence placed him at the scene of the crime. He was never charged.

You know how it is when a friend is in love. Well, I guess I'm talking to women, strong women, older women. (Sara was 60.) We say it's great being our own person, that our lives are full. But we still want it, recognize it. Romance. When Sara spun around my kitchen laughing, "I'm in love. Can you believe it?" I was glad for her. We all were. Leon was attractive. Well-educated, sexy, articulate. He made her happy. Later, as she did, we forgave him. Missed appointments, unkind words, thoughtlessness, a slap. We wanted everything to be OK. We all still wanted to believe in love.

After Sara's death her son Eddie moved into her house. I cleaned his house every Tuesday, so it turned out I was cleaning at Sara's. It was hard, at first, to be in her sunny kitchen with all the plants gone but the memories still there. Gossip, talks about God, our children. The living room was full of Eddie's CDs, radios and computers, two TVs, three telephones. (So much electronic equipment that once when the phone rang I answered it with the TV remote control.) His junky mismatched furniture replaced the huge linen couch where Sara and I would lie facing each other, covered with a quilt, talking, talking. Once one rainy Sunday we were both so low we watched bowling and *Lassie*.

The first time I cleaned the bedroom was terrible. The wall near where her bed used to be was still splattered and caked with her blood. I was sickened. After I cleaned it I went outside into the garden. I smiled to see the azaleas and daffodils and ranunculus we had planted together. We didn't know which end of the ranunculus to plant, so we decided to put in half of them with the point facing down and the other half with the point up. So we still don't know which are the ones that grew.

Our Brother's Keeper

I went back in to vacuum and make the bed, saw that under Eddie's bed was a revolver and a shotgun. I froze. What if Leon came back? He was crazy. He could kill me too. I took out each of the guns. Hands trembling, I tried to figure out what you did with them. I wanted Leon to come, so I could blow him away.

I vacuumed under the bed and put the weapons back. I was disgusted by my feelings and tried hard to think about something else.

I pretended that I was a TV show. A cleaning lady detective, sort of a female Columbo. Half-witted, gum chewing...but while she's feather dusting she's really looking for clues. She always just happens to be cleaning houses where a murder happens. Invisible, she mops the kitchen floor while suspects say incriminating things on the phone a few feet away. She eavesdrops, finds bloody knives in the linen cupboard, is careful not to dust the poker, saving prints...

Leon probably killed her with a golf club. That's how they met, at the Claremont Golf Club. I was scrubbing the bathtub when I heard the creak of the garden gate, a chair scraping on the wooden deck. Someone was in the back yard. Leon! My heart pounded. I couldn't see through the stained glass window. I crawled into the bedroom and grabbed the revolver, crawled to the french doors that led to the garden. I peeked out, gun ready, although my hand was shaking so bad I couldn't have shot it.

It was Alexander. Christ. Old Alexander, sitting in an Adirondack chair. Hi, Al! I called out, and went to put the gun away.

He was holding a clay pot of pink freesia that he kept meaning to bring to Sara. He had just felt like coming over to sit in her garden. I went in and poured him a cup of coffee. Sara had coffee going day and night. And good things to eat. Soups or gumbos, good bread and cheese and pastries. Not like the Winchell's donuts and frozen macaroni dinners Eddie kept around.

Alexander was an English professor. He could drone on for hours, Gerard Manley Hopkins gashing gold vermilion. He and

Sara had known each other for forty years, had been young idealistic socialists way back when. He had always been in love with her, would plead with her to marry him. Lorena and I used to beg her to do it. "Come on, Sara...let him take care of you." He was good. Noble and dependable. But, if a woman says a man is nice it usually means she finds him boring. And, like my mother used to say, "Ever tried being married to a saint?"

And that's just what Alexander was talking about...

"I was too boring for her, too predictable. I knew this chap was bad news. I only hoped that I would be around when he left, to help pick up the pieces."

Tears came into his eyes then. "I feel responsible for her death. I knew he had hurt her, would hurt her. I should have interfered some way. All I cared about was my own resentment and jealousy. I am guilty."

I held his hand and tried to cheer him up, and we talked for a while, remembering Sara.

After he had gone I went in to clean the kitchen. Hey, what if Alexander really was guilty? What if he had come over that night, with the pot of freesia, or to see if she wanted to play Scrabble? Maybe he had looked through the curtains on the french doors, seen Sara and Leon making love. He had waited until after Leon left, out the front door, and had gone in, wild with jealousy, and killed her. He was a suspect, for sure.

The next Tuesday the house wasn't as messy as usual so I spent the last hour weeding and replanting in the garden. I was in the potting shed when I heard the bells and tambourine. Hare Hare Hare. Sara's youngest daughter, Rebecca, was dancing and chanting around the swimming pool.

Sara had been upset at first, when she had become a Krishna, but one day we were driving down Telegraph and saw her among a group of them. She looked so beautiful, singing, bobbing around, in her saffron robes. Sara pulled the car over to the curb, just to sit and watch her. She lit a cigarette and smiled. "You know what? She's safe."

I tried to talk to Rebecca, get her to sit down and have some herbal tea or something, but she was spinning, spinning like a dervish, moaning away. Then she was jumping and twirling on the diving board, interrupting her chants with violent outbursts. "Evil begets evil!" She raved on about her mother's smoking and coffee drinking, about her eating red meat, and cheese with retin or something in it. And fornication. She was at the very tip of the diving board now, and every time she hollered "Fornication!" she'd bounce about three feet up into the air.

Suspect number two.

I only cleaned Eddie's once a week, but invariably at least one person came into the back yard. I'm sure people came in every other day as well. Because that's how she was, Sara, her heart and doors open to everyone. She helped in big ways, politically, in the community, but in little ways too, anyone who needed her. She always answered her phone, she never locked her doors. She had always been there for me.

One Tuesday, out of the blue, the biggest, worst suspect of all showed up in the back yard. Clarissa. Eddie's ex-girlfriend. Wow. I don't think she had ever been near Sara's house before, she hated her so much. She had tried to get Eddie to leave his mother's law firm, come live with her in Mendocino and be a full-time writer. She wrote letters to Sara, accusing her of being domineering and possessive, and fought with Eddie all the time about his law career and his mother. Clarissa and I had been friends until finally it came down to choosing between the two women. But not before I heard her say a hundred times, "Oh, how I'd love to murder Sara." And there she was, standing under the lavender wisteria that covered the gate, chewing on the stem of her dark glasses.

"Hi, Clarissa," I said.

She was startled. "Hi. I didn't expect to see anyone. What are you doing here?" (Typical of her...when in doubt, attack.)

"I'm cleaning Eddie's house."

"Are you still cleaning houses? That's sick."

"I sure hope you don't talk to your patients like that."

(Clarissa's a psychiatrist, for Lord's sake...) I tried hard to think of what questions my cleaning lady detective would ask her. I was at a loss, she was too intimidating. She really was *capable de tout*. How could I prove it, though?

"Where were you the night Sara was killed?" I blurted.

Clarissa laughed. "My dear... are you implying that I am guilty of the crime? No. Too late," she said as she turned and walked out of the gate.

As the weeks went by my list of suspects continued to grow, everyone from judges to policemen to window washers.

The only thing about the window washer was the weapon, the pole he carries around with him, along with his bucket. It was scary, seeing his silhouette through the curtains. A big man, carrying a pole. I had wondered about him for years. He is a homeless young black man who sleeps at night on Oakland busses and sometimes in the lobby of Alta Bates Emergency. During the day he goes from door to door asking people if they want their windows washed. He always has a book with him. Nathaniel Hawthorne. Jim Thompson. Karl Marx. He has a nice voice and dresses very well, tennis sweaters, Ralph Lauren T-shirts.

After Sara paid him for washing windows she'd always give him some god-awful old clothes of Eddie's. He'd say Thank you, ma'am, real polite, but I used to be sure he threw them in the garbage on his way out. Maybe she was a symbol or something. A jump suit with a broken zipper the last straw?

"Hello, Emory, how are you?"

"Just fine, and you? I saw that Miss Sara's son was living here now...wondered if he needed his windows washed."

Our Brother's Keeper

"No. I'm cleaning for him now, and do the windows too. Why don't you try at his office, on Prince Street?"

"Good idea. Thanks," he said. He smiled and left.

OK, I said to myself. Pull yourself together and cut this suspect business out right now.

I went in and got some coffee, went back to sit in the garden. Oh. The Japanese iris were in bloom. Sara, if only you could see them.

She had called me several times that day, telling me about his threats to her. I was impatient with her about Leon by then... why didn't she just break up with him? I listened to her and I said things like, call the police. Don't answer your phone.

When she called why didn't I say, "Come right on over to my house"? Why didn't I say, "Sara, pack your bag... Let's get out of town."

I have no alibi for the night of the crime.

Strays

Got into albuquerque from Baton Rouge. It was about two in the morning. Whipping wind. That's what the wind does in Albuquerque. I hung out at the Greyhound station until a cab driver showed up who had so many prison tattoos I figured I could score & he'd tell me where to stay. He turned me on, took me to a pad, a *noria* they call it there, in the south valley. I lucked out meeting him, Noodles. I couldn't have picked a worse place to run to than Albuquerque. Chicanos control the town. *Mayates*, they can't score at all, are lucky not to be killed. Some white guys, with enough long joint time to have been tested. White women, forget it, they don't last. Only way, and Noodles helped me there too, was to get hooked up with a big connection, like I did with Nacho. Then nobody could hurt me. What a pitiful thing I just said. Nacho was a saint, which may seem hard to believe. He did a lot for Brown Berets, for the whole Chicano community, young people, old people. I don't know where he is now. He skipped bail. I mean a huge bail. He shot a narc, Marquez, five times, in the back. The jury didn't think he was a saint, but Robin Hood maybe, because they only gave him manslaughter. I wish I knew where he was. I got busted about the same time, for needle marks.

All this happened many years ago or I couldn't even be talking about it. In those days you could end up with five or ten years for just a roach or marks.

So Long: Stories

It was when the first methadone rehabilitation programs were starting. I got sent to one of the pilot projects. Six months at La Vida instead of years in "la pinta," the state prison in Santa Fe. Twenty other addicts got the same deal. We all arrived in an old yellow school bus at La Vida. A pack of wild dogs met the bus, snarling and baying at us until finally they loped off into the dust.

La Vida was thirty miles out of Albuquerque. In the desert. Nothing around, not a tree, not a bush. Route 66 was too far to walk to. La Vida had been a radar site, a military installation during World War II. It had been abandoned since then. I mean abandoned. We were going to restore it.

We stood around in the wind, in the glare of the sun. Just the gigantic radar disc towering over the whole place, the only shade. Fallen down barracks. Torn and rusted venetian blinds rattling in the wind. Pin-ups peeled off the walls. Three or four foot sand dunes in every room. Dunes, with waves & patterns like in post cards from the Painted Desert.

A lot of things were going to contribute to our rehabilitation. Number one was removing us from the street environment. Every time a counselor said that we laughed ourselves silly. We couldn't see any roads, much less streets, and the streets in the compound were buried in sand. There were tables in the dining rooms and cots in the barracks but they were buried too. Toilets clogged with dead animals and more sand.

You could only hear the wind and the pack of dogs that kept circling. Sometimes it was nice, the silence, except the radar discs kept turning with a whining petty keening, day and night, day and night. At first it freaked us out, but after awhile it grew comforting, like wind chimes. They said it had been used to intercept Japanese kamikaze pilots, but they said a lot of pretty weird things.

Of course the major part of our rehab was going to be honest work. The satisfaction of a job well done. Learning to interact.

Strays

Teamwork. This teamwork started when we lined up for our methadone at six every morning. After breakfast we worked until lunchtime. Group from two until five, more group from seven to ten.

The purpose of these groups was to break us down. Our main problems were anger, arrogance, defiance. We lied and cheated and stole. There were daily "haircuts" where groups screamed at one person all his faults and weaknesses.

We were beaten down until we finally cried uncle. Who the fuck was uncle? See, I'm still angry, arrogant. I was ten minutes late to group & they shaved my eyebrows and cut my eyelashes.

The groups dealt with anger. All day long we dropped slips in a slip box saying who we were angry at and then in group we dealt with it. Mostly we just shouted what losers and fuck-ups everyone else was. But see, we all did lie and cheat. Half the time none of us was even mad, just shucking & jiving up some anger to play the group game, to stay at La Vida and not go to jail. Most of the slips were at Bobby, the cook, for feeding those wild dogs. Or things like Greñas doesn't weed enough, he just smokes and pushes tumbleweeds around with a rake.

We were mad at those dogs. Lines of us at six a.m. and at one and six outside the dining room. Whipping sand wind. We'd be tired and hungry. Freezing in the morning and hot in the afternoon. Bobby would wait, finally stroll across his floor like a smug bank official to unlock the door for us. And while we waited, a few feet away, at the kitchen door, the dogs would be waiting too, for him to throw them slops. Mangy, motley, ugly dogs people had abandoned out on the mesa. The dogs liked Bobby all right but they hated us, baring their teeth & snarling, day after day, meal after meal.

I got moved from the laundry to the kitchen. Helping cook, dishwashing and mopping up. I felt better about Bobby after a while. I even felt better about the dogs. He named them all. Dumb names. Duke, Spot, Blackie, Gimp, Shorty. And Liza, his favorite. An old yellow cur, flat-headed, with huge bat-like ears and amber yellow eyes. After a few months she'd even eat out of his hand. "Sunshine! Liza, my yellow-eyed sun," he used to croon to her. Finally she let him scratch behind her ugly ears and just above the long ratty tail that hung down between her legs. "My sweet sweet sunshine," he'd say.

Government money kept sending in people to do workshops with us. A lady who did a workshop about Families. As if any of us ever had a family. And some guy from Synanon who said our problem was our cool. His favorite expression was "When you think you're looking good you're looking bad." Every day he had us "blow our image." Which was just acting like fools.

We got a gym and a pool table, weights and punching bags. Two color televisions. A basketball court, a bowling alley and a tennis court. Framed paintings by Georgia O'Keeffe. Monet's "Waterlilies." Soon a Hollywood movie company was coming, to make a science fiction film at the site. We would be able to work as extras and make some money. The movie was going to center around the radar disc & what it did to Angie Dickinson. It fell in love with her and took her soul when she died in a car wreck. It would take over all these other live souls, too, who would be La Vida residents, us. I've seen it about twenty times, in the middle of the night, on TV.

All in all the first three months went pretty well. We were clean and healthy; we worked hard. The site was in great shape. We got pretty close to each other and we did get angry. But for those first three months we were in total isolation. Nobody came in and nobody went out. No phone calls, no newspapers, no mail, no television. Things started falling apart when that ended. People went on passes and had dirty urines when they got back, or they didn't come back at all. New residents kept coming in, but they didn't have the sense of pride we had about the place.

Every day we had a morning meeting. Part gripe session, part snitch session. We also had to take turns speaking, even if it was just telling a joke or singing a song. But nobody could ever think of anything, so at least twice a week old Lyle Tanner sang "I thought I saw a whip-poor-will." "El Sapo" gave a talk on how to breed chihuahuas, which was gross. Sexy kept on reciting the 23rd psalm. Only the way she caressed words it sounded lewd and everybody laughed, which hurt her feelings.

Sexy's name was a joke. She was an old whore from Mexico. She hadn't come with the first group of us, but later, after five days in solitary with no food. Bobby made her soup and some bacon and eggs. But all she wanted was bread. She sat there & ate three loaves of Wonder bread, not even chewing it, just swallowing it, famished. Bobby gave the soup and bacon and eggs to Liza.

Sexy kept on eating until finally I took her to our room and she collapsed. Lydia and Sherry were in bed together in the next room. They had been lovers for years. I could tell by their slow laughs that they were high on something, reds or ludes probably. I went back to the kitchen to help Bobby clean up. Gabe, the counselor, came in to get the knives, to lock them up in the safe. He did that every night.

"I'm going to town. You're in charge, Bobby." There never were any staff members at night anymore.

Bobby and I went out to drink coffee under the chinaberry tree. The dogs yelped after something on the mesa.

"I'm glad Sexy came. She's nice."

"She's ok. She won't stay."

"She reminds me of Liza."

"Liza's not that ugly. Oye, Tina, be still. It's almost here."

The moon. There's no other moon like one on a clear New Mexico night. It rises over the Sandias and soothes the miles and miles of barren desert with all the quiet whiteness of a first snow. Moonlight in Liza's yellow eyes and the chinaberry tree.

The world just goes along. Nothing much matters, you know?

I mean really matters. But then sometimes, just for a second, you get this grace, this belief that it does matter, a whole lot.

He felt that way too. I heard the catch in his throat. Some people may have said a prayer, knelt down, at a moment like that. Sung a hymn. Maybe cavemen would have done a dance. What we did was make love. "El Sapo" busted us. Later, but we were still naked.

So it came out at morning meeting and we had to get a punishment. Three weeks, after cleaning the kitchen, to strip and sand all the paint around the dining room windows. Until one in the morning, every single night. That was bad enough but then Bobby, trying to save his ass, got up and said, "I didn't want to ball Tina. I just want to stay clean, do my time and go home to my wife Debbi and my baby Debbi-Ann." I could have dropped a slip on those two jive names.

That hurt bad. He had held me and talked to me. He had gone to a lot more trouble making love than most men do and I had been happy with him when the moon came up.

We had to work so hard there wasn't time to talk. I would never have let him know how bad it hurt anyway. We were tired, bone tired every night, all day.

The main thing we hadn't talked about was the dogs. They hadn't shown up for three nights.

Finally I said it. "Where do you think the dogs are?"

He shrugged. "A puma. Kids with guns."

We went back to sanding. It got too late even to go to bed so we made some fresh coffee and sat down under the tree.

I missed Sexy. I forgot to say that she had gone to town to the dentist but had managed to score, got busted and taken back to jail.

"I miss Sexy. Bobby, that was a lie what you said at morning meeting. You did so want to ball me."

"Yeah, it was a lie."

We went into the meat locker & held each other again, made

Strays

love again but not for long because it was freezing cold. We went back outside.

The dogs starting coming. Shorty, Blackie, Spot, Duke.

They had gotten into porcupines. Must have been days ago because they were all so infected, septic. Their faces swollen like monster rhinoceros, oozing green pus. Their eyes were bloated shut, quilled shut with tiny arrows. That was the scary part, that none of them could see. Or make a real sound since their throats were engorged too.

Blackie had a seizure. Hurtled up into the air with an eerie gargle. Thrashing, jerking, peeing in the air. High, two, three feet into the air and then he fell wet, dead, into the dust. Liza came in last because she couldn't walk, just crawled until she got to Bobby's feet, writhed there, her paw patting at his boot.

"Get me the goddam knives."

"Gabe's not back yet." Only counselors could unlock the safe.

Liza pawed at Bobby's foot, gentle, like asking to be petted, for him to throw her a ball.

Bobby went to the locker and brought out a steak. The sky was lavender. It was almost morning.

He had the dogs smell the meat. He called to them, cooed to them to follow him across the road to the machine shop. I stayed under the tree.

When he was in there, when he finally got them all in there, he beat them to death with a sledge hammer. I didn't see it, but I heard it and from where I sat I saw the blood splattering and streaking down the walls. I thought he would say something like "Liza, my sweet sunshine" but he didn't say a word. When he came out he was covered in blood, didn't look at me, went to the barracks.

The nurse drove up with the doses of methadone and everybody started lining up for breakfast. I turned the griddle on and started making batter. Everybody was mad because I took so long with breakfast.

There still wasn't any staff around when the movie trailers started pulling in. They began working right away, checking out locations, casting extras. People were running around with megaphones and walkie-talkies. Somehow nobody went into the machine shop.

They started one scene right away...a take of a stunt man who was supposed to be Angie Dickinson driving down from the gym while a helicopter hovered around the radar disc. The car was supposed to crash into the disc and Angie's spirit fly up into it but the car crashed into the chinaberry tree.

Bobby and I made lunch, so tired we were walking in slow motion, just like all the zombie extras were being told to walk. We didn't talk. Once, making tuna salad I said out loud, to myself, "Pickle relish?"

"What did you say?"

"I said pickle relish."

"Christ. Pickle relish!" We laughed, couldn't stop laughing. He touched my cheek, lightly, a bird's wing.

The movie crew thought the radar site was Fab, far out. Angie Dickinson liked my eye shadow. I told her it was just chalk, the kind you rub on pool cues. "It's to die for, that blue," she said to me.

After lunch, an old gaffer, whatever that is, came up to me and asked where the nearest bar was. There was a place up the road, toward Gallup, but I told him Albuquerque. I told him I would do anything to get a ride into town.

"Don't worry about that. Hop in my truck and let's go."

Wham, crash, bang.

"Good God, what was that?" he asked.

"A cattle guard."

"Jesus, this sure is one godforsaken place."

We finally hit the highway. It was great, the sound of tires on the cement, the wind blowing in. Semis, bumper stickers, kids fighting in the back seats. Route 66.

Strays

We got to the rise, with the wide valley and the Rio Grande below us, the Sandia mountains lovely above.

"Mister, what I need is money for a ticket home to Baton Rouge. Can you spare it, about sixty dollars?"

"Easy. You need a ticket. I need a drink. It will all work out."

Fire

My sister is dying of cancer. I usually just call her Sally but now I keep saying my sister.

I wait for the flight to Mexico City. Maybe she's exaggerating, as usual. Maybe I won't get there in time. Maybe she will live a year, and here I've just quit my job. The Mexicana flight crew heads toward the entrance. Not like American pilots who just go get on the plane. First the pilot himself, moustache and white scarf, his raincoat dragging like a matador's cape. Two paces behind, banderillero copilots and then the male flight attendants, in step. Reluctantly follow the sleepy, heavily made-up stewardesses. Glamorous, hating to come back to work. It's only Americans who smile unnecessarily.

Sally, you were so little when we first went to Mexico City, by train, when all the volcanoes were vast and visible against the blue sky.

My sister married in Mexico and never left. We had different lives. Not really. Differently alone. Our parents dead now, husbands gone, children grown.

She was born just before Daddy went to war and we moved to Texas to Mamie's. He was gone. Everybody doted on her, the sweet one. I think I must have hated her; I don't remember her then at all.

On the train from Spokane to Texas you were a month old, asleep in a drawer Mama took from the bureau of the Davenport

hotel. She laughed because it fit you perfectly. The train was
wonderful, the noisy vestibules, the upper bunk and a hammock
for shoes but I was frightened by Mama taking the drawer. In
the bathroom she vomited and vomited. I put a rag on her head.
The toilet opened onto the ground. Green grass and dandelions.
Railroad ties, ties, ties speeding on and on below her wet head.
She sang, to the tune of "Humoresque": "I wish people would
refrain/ from flushing toilets on the train/ while train is in the
station/ I love you!" She changed you and gave you a bottle. You
slept in the drawer. I was hungry. She drank and then she slept
and I couldn't wake her. The train clanked and hissed, backed
up, coupled. Men laughed on the platform. Lanterns arced
amber through the frosted glass. We lurched away again, faster
and faster. You both slept on, but I was afraid you would wake
up and cry. I couldn't go to sleep. I mean, I had to stay awake.

The porter came in. He was tiny but frightening because I had
never seen black people before. Come along to bed, now, miss,
never you mind.

In the morning you were smiling. Blue baby eyes. Now they
are green, the color of Oaxacan jade. Clear open eyes, always
trusting. You never expected anything to go wrong. I always
did. When I woke up, on the train, there was Mama all fresh
and combed and putting on lipstick. Look at the pretty cows!
Moo-cows, Sally!

No tourists on this flight. Mexican families with videos, wal-
kmans, microwaves. The pilot speaks over the loudspeaker, not
to tell us the location or altitude but to say he's turning off the
lights for a while. Please, everybody, go look at the sunset on
the right side of the aircraft. Blazing reds, magentas, streaks of
ocher yellow in swirls of clouds. Everyone rushes to the right
side of the plane. Except me, I'm afraid it will tip.

The movie *Big* goes back on and the stewardesses, charming
and festive now, pass cheese and fruit, champagne. You can
still smoke on Mexican planes so I smoke and smoke. Sally,

Fire

I am surprised by the pain of losing you, by the gash of it. The movie goes off again, the pilot says he's turning out the lights once more. Please, immediately, look at the moon to the left of the plane! A full orange moon rises over the mountains above Puerto Vallarta. He forgets to turn the movie or the lights back on. We fly along, silent in the dark, looking at the moon as the plane begins the descent into Mexico City. Flaps down. The plane cuts through a thick tarpaulin of smog and fecal dust and the dazzle of the city explodes for miles around us. The plane thuds and bounces careening into a terrifying landing. Passengers and two stewardesses make the sign of the cross.

Will someone meet me? Do I take a cab? A long wait for the luggage. Sheets, feather pillows, presents for Sally's children. Two very expensive wigs for Sally's bald head. Your red curling hair. Admit it, this must be awful, awful, to lose your lovely hair. At last the bags arrive. A *mozo* loads them onto a cart and runs toward the exit. I run after him, think he's stealing them. I can't breathe, the high altitude, the acrid smell. We rush past customs. The *mozo* drops the bags, grabs my tip and keeps on running.

Inside the barrier is my sister. But Sally, it is just like you as a child, your tiny head in a cap like a baby hat. Small, you got so small but your eyes are wide and green. A horrible grimace of terror upon your face. The surly man next to you wears the same expression. But everyone is running now and you are both screaming at me. I kick the bags along the floor. My back ... I can't carry them. Screaming, screaming. The man comes for the bags, but drops them.

The airport is on fire! I'll get the car. Run!

We wrap shawls around our faces. You pick up the heaviest two suitcases and trot clumsily ahead of me. You turn once to see if I'm following. Sweat pours from your bony face. How can you be so strong? My chest aches, I can't breathe, running after you. Tendrils of green smoke slide around our necks. Two women collapse onto the marble floor. A boy grabs at the bag

So Long: Stories

I carry. I kick him away. Smoke is yellow-black, blinding. All the lights go out. I have lost you. I run, sobbing; I see your skull. Your cap has gone and you sit on the bags like a sleepy baby. Your head shines pink, new. You are across the *avenida*, crumpled onto the curb. A policeman tries to make you move. You can't move. Another boy tries to get the bag you sit on. *Vayase, pendejo!* You smile at me. Did we save the wigs? Police are making everyone run to safety. No, too dangerous to get to parking. Airplane tanks might explode any minutes. Your ex-husband is in the President's cabinet; his car will surely get through. Yellow flares cascade on the divider. Ambulances are loading people who have been trampled, who have fallen from the fumes.

It is bright now because of the bursts of gay yellow flames and flashing red lights. Gusts of unbearably hot air sweep at us. Except for the sirens it is eerily still. A rustle of fire, quiet, thickening vines of smoke.

The Mercedes-Benz appears, flags flying. The policeman notices that you are very ill, lifts you into the air. Just folds you all up and puts you in. The crowd, their faces covered, stare at the lone limousine, the two laughing women. We speed away, the car buckles and spins from the impact of the explosion behind us. Ghastly yellow green pulsations, belches of fire.

Señora, are you all right? the chauffeur asks.

I'm frightened. We are frightened!

Fíjese, no más ... the sirens are all going the other way!

The car glides down the *periferico*, going 100. Neon lights dart past like underwater fish through the black windows. Muted cacophony of sirens as ambulances pass us on both sides.

Carlotta, we have had so many adventures! you say.

Dangers!

The ship off Panama.

Grandpa.

Grandpa!

Fire

The biplane was the worst, in Chile. Through those ravines in an open cockpit. God, we are old. That plane was made of paper!

Canvas. He was handsome, remember? What a death!

Shortly after, the pilot crashed the same plane into the side of the Andes above Santiago. The burnt outline of the aircraft stood out clearly against the mountain until the rains finally came and grass grew to cover it.

Carlotta . . . We only met him for half an hour, but you stared out the window at that plane print and sobbed for at least six months!

I wasn't crying for him, Sally. It was the imprint of the plane. God, she never understands anything, really.

You are holding my hand with yours. I don't know your hands now. I kiss you softly.

Carlotta, isn't this a wonderful car? Air-tight, sound-proof, bulletproof. I want to be buried in it.

I don't like it much. Weird to be in Mexico and not be able to smell it. Seriously though, I've thought about this coffin problem. Mexicans adore plastic. Tupperware coffins! All sizes. I could make a killing.

You enclose me in a brittle embrace, a carapace.

I knew you would come and make me laugh.

We always laugh. It's a family tic. This isn't funny, Sally. Please, let's don't laugh now.

I have said the right thing. You sigh and let go, sinking back into the velvet, your face slack-jawed with exhaustion. Your eyes look into mine.

Whatever will you do without me?

What will I do? A sick moan surges up from my body into a cry. And Sally, you always copy everything I do. You cry out too. The unison of our wail comes from far away, deep, from where we first knew one another.

The limousine speeds on, cool and silent, down Avenida de Los Insurgentes. My sister and I fall asleep.

Melina

In Albuquerque, in the evening, my husband Rex would go to class at the university or to his sculpture studio. I took Ben, the baby, for long walks in his stroller. Up the hill, on a street leafy with elm trees was Clyde Tingley's house. We always went past that house. Clyde Tingley was a millionaire who gave all his money to children's hospitals in the state. We went by his house because not just at Christmas but all the time he had Christmas tree lights strung up, all over the porch and on all the trees. He would turn them on just as it was dusk, as we were on the way home. Sometimes he would be in his wheelchair on the porch, a skinny old man who would holler "Hello" and "Lovely evening" to us as we passed. One night though he yelled at me "Stop! Stop! Something wrong with that there child's feet! Need to be seen to."

I looked down at Ben's feet, which were fine.

"No, it's because he's too big for the stroller now. He's just holding them up funny so they won't drag on the ground."

Ben was so smart. He didn't even talk yet but he seemed to understand. He set his feet squarely on the ground, as if to show the old man they were ok.

"Mothers never want to admit there's any problem. You take him to a doctor now."

Just then a man dressed all in black walked up. Even then you rarely saw people out walking so he was a surprise. He was squatting on the sidewalk holding Ben's feet in his hands. A saxophone strap dangled from his neck and Ben grabbed at it.

"No, sir. Nothing wrong with this boy's feet," he said.

"Well, I'm glad to hear it," Clyde Tingley called.

"Thanks, anyway," I said.

The man and I stood there talking, and then he walked us home. This happened in 1956; he was the first beatnik I ever met. There hadn't been anyone like him that I had seen in Albuquerque. Jewish, with a Brooklyn accent. Long hair and a beard, dark glasses. But he didn't seem sinister. Ben liked him right away. His name was Beau. He was a poet and a musician, played saxophone. It was later I found out that it was a saxophone strap hanging from his neck.

We became friends right away. He played with the baby while I made iced tea. After I put Ben to bed we sat outside on the porch steps talking until Rex came home. The two men were polite to each other but didn't get along too well, I could see that right away. Rex was a graduate student. We were really poor then, but Rex seemed like someone older and powerful. An air of success, maybe a little conceit. Beau acted like he didn't much care about anything, which I already knew wasn't true. After he left Rex said he didn't like the idea of me dragging home stray hep-cats.

Beau was hitchhiking his way home to New York…the Apple…after six months in San Francisco. He was staying with friends, but they worked all day, so he came to see me and Ben every day, the four days he was there.

Beau really needed to talk. It was wonderful for me to hear somebody talk, besides Ben's few words, so I was glad to see him. Besides, he talked about romance. He had fallen in love. Now I knew that Rex loved me, and we were happy, would have a happy life together, but he wasn't madly in love with me the way Beau was with Melina.

Beau had been a sandwich man in San Francisco. He had a little cart with sweet rolls and coffee, soft drinks and sandwiches.

Melina

He pushed it up and down the floors of a gigantic office building. One day he had pulled his cart into an insurance office and he saw her. Melina. She was filing, but not really filing, looking out the window with a dreamy smile on her face. She had long dyed blonde hair and wore a black dress. She was very tiny and thin. But it was her skin, he said. It was like she wasn't a person at all but some creature made of white silk, of milk glass.

Beau didn't know what came over him. He left the cart and his customers, went through a little gate over to where she stood. He told her he loved her. I want you, he said. I'll get the bathroom key. Come on. It will just take five minutes. Melina looked at him and said, I'll be right there.

I was pretty young then. This was the most romantic thing I had ever heard.

Melina was married and had a baby girl about a year old. Ben's age. Her husband was a trumpet player. He was on the road for the two months Beau knew Melina. They had a passionate affair and when her husband was coming home she said to Beau, "Time to hit the road." So he did.

Beau said you had to do anything she said, that she cast a spell on him, on her husband, on any man who knew her. You couldn't get jealous, he said, because it seemed perfectly natural that any other man would love her.

For example...the baby wasn't even her husband's. For a while they had been living in El Paso. Melina worked at Piggly Wiggly packing meat and chickens and sealing them in plastic. Behind a glass window, in a funny paper hat. But still this Mexican bullfighter who was buying steaks saw her. He banged on the counter and rang a bell, insisted to the butcher that he see the wrapping woman. He made her leave work. That's how she affected you, Beau said. You had to be near her immediately.

A few months later Melina realized she was pregnant. She was really happy, and told her husband. He was furious. You can't be, he said, I had a vasectomy. What? Melina was indignant.

And you married me without telling me this? She kicked him out of the house, changed the locks. He sent flowers, wrote her passionate letters. He camped out outside the door until at last she forgave him for what he did.

She sewed all their clothes. She had covered all the rooms in the apartment with fabric. There were mattresses and pillows on the floors so you crawled, like a baby, from tent to tent. In candlelight day and night you never knew what time it was.

Beau told me everything about Melina. About her childhood in foster homes, how she ran away at thirteen. She was a B-girl in a bar (I'm not sure what that is) and her husband had rescued her from a very ugly situation. She's tough, Beau said, she talks nasty. But her eyes, her touch, they are like an angel child's. She was this angel that just came into my life and ruined it forever… He did get dramatic about her, and even cried and cried sometimes, but I loved hearing all about her, wished I could be like her. Tough, mysterious, beautiful.

I was sorry when Beau left. He was like an angel in my life, too. When he was gone I realized how little Rex ever talked to me or Ben. I felt so lonely I even thought about turning our rooms into tents.

« · »

A few years later I was married to a different man, a jazz piano player named David. He was a good man but he was quiet too. I don't know why I married those quiet guys, when the thing I like best in the world to do is to talk. We had a lot of friends though. Musicians coming into town would stay with us and while the men played we women cooked and talked and lay around on the grass playing with the kids.

It was like pulling teeth to get David to tell me what he was like in first grade, or about his first girlfriend, anything. I knew he had lived with a woman, a beautiful painter, for five years, but he didn't want to talk about her. Hey, I said, I've told you my whole life story, tell me something about you, tell me when you first fell in love... He laughed then, but he actually told me. That's easy, he said.

It was a woman who was living with his best friend, a bass player, Ernie Jones. Down in the south valley, by the irrigation ditch. Once he had gone to see Ernie and when he wasn't home he went down to the ditch.

She was sun-bathing, naked and white against the green grass. For sunglasses she wore those paper lace doilies they put under ice cream.

"So. That's it?" I prodded.

"Well, yeah. That's it. I fell in love."

"But what was she like?"

"She wasn't like anyone in this world. Once Ernie and I were lying around by the ditch, talking, smoking weed. We were real blue because we were both out of work. She was supporting us both, working as a waitress. One day she worked a noon banquet and she brought all the flowers home, a whole roomful. But what she did was carry them all upstream and dump them in the ditch. So Ernie and I were sitting there, gloomy, on the bank, staring at the muddy water and then a billion flowers floated by. She had taken food and wine, even silver and tablecloths that she set up on the grass."

"So, did you make love with her?"

"No. I never even talked to her, alone anyway. I just—remember her—in the grass."

"Hm," I said, pleased by all that information and by the sort of sappy look on his face. I loved romance in any form.

« · »

We moved to Santa Fe, where David played piano at Claude's. A lot of good musicians passed through town in those years and would sit in with David's trio for one or two nights. Once a really good trumpet player came, Paco Duran. David liked playing with him, and asked if it was ok with me if Paco and his wife and child stayed with us for a week. Sure, I said, it will be nice.

It was. Paco played great. He and David played all night at work and together all day at home. Paco's wife, Melina, was exotic and fun. They talked and acted like L.A. jazz musicians. Called our house a pad and said "you dig?" and "outta sight." Their little girl and Ben got along great but were both at the age where they got into everything. We tried putting them both in a playpen but neither one of them would go for it. Melina got the idea that we should just let them carry on and she and I should get inside the playpen with our coffee and ashtrays safe. So there we were, sitting in there while the kids took books out of the bookcase. She was telling me about Las Vegas, making it sound like another planet. I realized, listening to her, not just looking at her but being surrounded by her other-worldly beauty, that this was Beau's Melina.

Somehow I couldn't say anything about it. I couldn't say Hey, you are so beautiful and weird you must be Beau's romance. But I thought of Beau and missed him, hoped he was doing fine.

She and I cooked dinner and the men went off to work. We bathed the children and went out on the back porch, smoked and drank coffee, talked about shoes. We talked about all the important shoes in our lives. The first penny loafers, first high heels. Silver platforms. Boots we had known. Perfect pumps. Handmade sandals. Huaraches. Spike heels. While we talked our bare feet wriggled in the damp green grass by the porch. Her toenails were painted black.

She asked me what my sign was. Usually this annoyed me but I let her tell me everything about my Scorpio self and I believed every word. I told her I read palms, a little, and looked at her

Melina

hands. It was too dark so I went in and got a kerosene lantern, set it on the steps between us. I held her two white hands by lantern and moonlight, and remembered what Beau had said about her skin. It was like holding cool glass, silver.

I know Cheiro's palmistry book by heart. I have read hundreds of palms. I'm telling you this so you'll know I did tell her things that I saw in the lines and mounds of her hands. But mostly I told her everything Beau had told me about her.

I'm ashamed of why I did this. I was jealous of her. She was so dazzling. She didn't really do anything special, her *being* dazzled. I wanted to impress her.

I told her her life story. I told her about the horrible foster parents, how Paco protected her. Said things like, "I see a man. Handsome man. Danger. You are not in danger. He is in danger. A race driver, bullfighter maybe?" Fuck, she said, nobody knew about the bullfighter.

Beau had told me that once he put his hand on her head and said "It will all be all right..." and she had wept. I told her that she never ever cried, not when she was sad or mad. But that if someone was really kind and just put their hand on her head and said not to worry, that might make her cry...

I won't tell you any more. I'm too ashamed. But it had exactly the effect I had intended. She sat there staring at her beautiful hands and she whispered, "You are a witch. You are magic."

We had a wonderful week. We all went to Indian dances and climbed in Bandolier monument and Acoma pueblo. We sat in the cave where Sandia man had lived. We soaked in hot springs near Taos and went to the church of the Santo Niño. Two nights we even got a baby sitter so Melina and I could go to the club. The music was great. "I have had a wonderful time this week," I said. She smiled, "I always have a wonderful time," she said, simply.

The house was very quiet when they had gone. I woke up, as usual, when David came home. I think I wanted to confess to him about the palm reading, but I'm glad I didn't. We were lying in bed together in the dark when he said to me,

"That was her."

"That was who?"

"Melina. She was the woman in the grass."

Step

The West Oakland detox used to be a warehouse. It is dark inside and echoes like an underground parking lot. Bedrooms, a kitchen and the office open off of a vast room. In the middle of the room is a pool table and the TV pit. They call it the pit because the walls around it are only five feet high, so the counselors can look down into it.

Most of the residents were in the pit, in blue pajamas, watching *Leave it to Beaver*. Bobo held a cup of tea for Carlotta to drink. The other men were laughing about her running around the train yard, trying to go under the engine. The Amtrak from L.A. had stopped. Carlotta laughed too. All of them running around in pajamas. Not that she didn't care about what she had done. She didn't remember, didn't own the deed at all.

Milton, a counselor, came to the rim of the pit.

"When's the fight?"

"Two hours." Benitez and Sugar Ray Leonard for the welterweight title.

"Sugar Ray will take it, easy." Milton grinned at Carlotta and the men made comments, jokes. She knew most of the men from other times here, from detoxes in Hayward, Richmond, San Francisco. Bobo she knew from Highland psych ward too.

All twenty of the residents were in the pit now, with pillows and blankets, huddled together like pre-school kids at nap time, Henry Moore drawings of people in bomb shelters. On the

TV Orson Welles said "We sell no wine before its time." Bobo laughed, "It's time, brother, it's time!"

"Stop your shakin, woman, messes the TV."

A man with dreadlocks sat down beside Carlotta, put his hand inside her thigh. Bobo grabbed the man's wrist. "Move it or I'll break it." Old Sam came in wrapped in a blanket. There was no heat and it was bitterly cold.

"Sit there on her feets. You can hold them still."

Cheaper by the Dozen was almost over. Clifton Webb died and Myrna Loy went to college. Willie said he had liked it in Europe because white people were ugly there. Carlotta didn't know what he meant, then realized that the only people that solitary drunks ever see are on television. At three in the morning she would wait to see Jack the Ripper for Used Datsuns. Slashin them prices. Jest a hackin and a hewin.

The television was the only light in the detox. It was as if the pit were their own smoky ring, with the boxing ring inside it in color. The announcer's voice was shrill. Tonight's purse is one million dollars! All the men had their money on Sugar Ray, would have had. Bobo told Carlotta some of the men there weren't even alcoholics, had just faked needing detox so they could watch the fight.

Carlotta was for Benitez. You likes them pretty boys, Mama? Benitez was pretty, with fine bones, a dapper moustache. He weighed 144 pounds, had won his first championship at seventeen. Sugar Ray Leonard was scarcely heavier but he seemed to tower, not moving. The men met in the center of the ring. There was no sound. The crowd on TV, the residents in the pit held their breath as the boxers faced each other, circling, sinuous, their eyes locked.

In the third round Leonard's quick hook knocked Benitez to the ground. He was up in a second, with a child-like smile. Embarrassed. I didn't mean for that to happen to me. At that moment the men in the pit began to want him to win.

Step

No one moved, not even during the commercials. Sam rolled cigarettes all through the fight, passed them. Milton came up to the ledge of the pit during the sixth round, just as Benitez took a blow to the forehead, his only mark in the fight. Milton saw the blood reflected in everyone's eyes, in their sweat.

"Figures...you'd all be backing a loser," he said.

"Quiet! Round eight."

"Come on, baby, don't you go down."

They weren't asking Benitez to win, just to stay in the fight. He did, he stayed in. He retreated in the ninth behind a jab, then a left hook drove him into the ropes and a right knocked out his mouthpiece.

Round ten, round eleven, round twelve, round thirteen, round fourteen. He stayed in. No one in the pit spoke. Sam had fallen asleep.

The bell rang for the last round. The arena was so quiet you could hear Sugar Ray Leonard whisper. "Oh, my God. He is still standing."

But Benitez's right knee touched the canvas. Briefly, like a Catholic leaving a pew. The slightest deference that meant the flight was over; he had lost. Carlotta whispered,

"God, please help me."

Fool to Cry

Solitude is an Anglo-Saxon concept. In Mexico City, if you're the only person on a bus and someone gets on they'll not only come next to you, they will lean against you.

When my sons were at home, if they came into my room there was usually a specific reason. Have you seen my socks? What's for dinner? Even now, when the bell on my gate rings it will be Hi, Ma! let's go to the A's game, or Can you baby-sit tonight? But in Mexico, my sister's daughters will come up three flights of stairs and through three doors just because I am there. To lean against me or say *Qué honda?*

Their mother Sally is sleeping soundly; she has taken pain pills and a sleeping pill. She doesn't hear me, in the bed next to hers, turning pages, coughing. When Tino, her fifteen-year-old son, comes home he gives me a kiss, goes to her bed and lies next to her, holds her hand. He kisses her goodnight and goes to his room.

Mercedes and Victoria live in their own apartment across town, but every night they stop by even though she doesn't wake up. Victoria smooths Sally's brow, arranges her pillows and blankets, draws a star on her bald head with a felt-tip pen. Sally moans in her sleep, wrinkles her brow. Hold still, *Amor*, Victoria says. About four in the morning Mercedes comes to say goodnight to her mother. She is a set designer for movies. When she's working she works day and night. She too lies against Sally, sings to her, kisses her head. She sees the star and she laughs. Victoria has been here! Tia, are you awake? *Sí. Oye!* let's go smoke. We got into the kitchen. She is very tired, dirty. Stands staring into the refrigerator, sighs and closes it. We smoke and share an apple, sitting together on the only chair in the kitchen. She is happy. The film they are making is wonderful, the director is the best. She is doing a good job. "They treat me with respect, like a man! Cappelini wants me to work on his next movie!"

In the morning Sally and Tino and I go to La Vega for coffee. Tino carries his cappuccino with him as he goes from table to table, talking with friends, flirting with girls. Mauricio the chauffeur waits outside, to take Tino to school. Sally and I talk and talk, as we have since I arrived from California three days before. She is wearing a curly auburn wig, a green dress that enhances her jade eyes. Everyone stares at her, fascinated. Sally has come to this café for twenty-five years. Everyone knows she is dying, but she has never looked so beautiful or happy.

Now, me... if they said I had a year to live, I'll bet I would just swim out to sea, get it over with. But Sally, it is as if the sentence had been a gift. Maybe it's because she fell in love with Xavier the week before she found out. She has come alive. She savors everything. She says whatever she wants, does whatever makes her feel good. She laughs. Her walk is sexy, her voice is sexy. She gets mad and throws things, hollers cuss words. Little Sally, always meek and passive, in my shadow as a girl, in her husband's for most of her life. She is strong, radiant now; her zest is contagious. People stop by the table to greet her, men kiss her hand. The doctor, the architect, the widower.

Mexico City is a huge metropolis but people have titles, like the blacksmith in a village. The medical student; the judge; Victoria, the ballerina; Mercedes, the beauty; Sally's ex-husband, the minister. I am the American sister. Everyone greets me with hugs and cheek kisses.

Fool to Cry

Sally's ex-husband, Ramon, stops in for an espresso, shadowed by bodyguards. Chairs scrape back all over the restaurant as men stand to shake his hand or give him an *abrazo*. He is a cabinet member now, for the PRI. He kisses Sally and me, asks Tino about his school. Tino hugs his father goodbye and leaves for class. Ramon looks at his watch.

Wait a little bit, Sally says. They want so badly to see you; they are sure to come.

Victoria first, in a low-cut leotard on her way to dance class. Her hair is punk; she has a tattoo on her shoulder. For God's sake, cover yourself! her father says.

"Papi, everybody here is used to me, no, Julian?"

Julian, the waiter, shakes his head. "No, *mi doña*, each day you bring us a new surprise."

He has brought us all what we wanted without taking an order. Tea for Sally, a second latte for me, an espresso, then a latte, for Ramon.

Mercedes arrives, her hair wild, her face heavily made-up, on the way to a modeling job before going to the movie set. Everyone in the café has known Victoria and Mercedes since they were babies, but stares at them nonetheless because they are so beautiful, so scandalously dressed.

Ramon starts his usual lecture. Mercedes has appeared in some sexy scenes for Mexican MTV. An embarrassment. He wants Victoria to go to college and get a part-time job. She puts her arms around him.

"Now, Papi, why should I go to school, when all I want to do is dance? And why should I work, when we are so rich?"

Ramon shakes his head, and ends up giving her money for her lessons, more for some shoes, more for a cab, since she's late. She leaves, waving goodbyes and blowing kisses to the café.

Ramon groans. "I'm late!" He leaves too, weaving through a gauntlet of hand-shakes. A black limousine speeds him away, down Insurgentes.

"*Pues,* finally we can eat," Mercedes says. Julian arrives with juice and fruit and *chilaquiles.* "Mamá, could you try something, just a little?" Sally shakes her head. She has chemo later, and it makes her sick.

"I didn't sleep a wink last night!" Sally says. She looks hurt when Mercedes and I laugh, but she laughs, too, when we tell her all the people she slept through.

"Tomorrow is Tía's birthday. Basil day!" Mercedes said. "Mamá, were you at the Grange Fête, too?"

"Yes, but I was little, only seven, the time it fell on Carlotta's twelfth birthday, the year she met Basil. Everybody was there … grown-ups, children. There was a little English world within the country of Chile. Anglican churches and English manors and cottages. English gardens and dogs. The Prince of Wales Country Club. Rugby and cricket teams. And of course the Grange school. A very good Eton-type boys' school."

"And all the girls at our school were in love with Grange boys…"

"The Fête lasted all day. There were soccer and cricket games and cross-country races, shot-put and jumping events. All kinds of games and booths, things to buy and to eat."

"Fortune tellers," Carlotta said. "She told me I would have many lovers and many troubles."

"I could have told you that. Anyway, it was just like an English country fair."

"What did he look like?"

"Noble and worried. Tall and handsome, except for rather large ears."

"And a lantern jaw…"

"Late in the afternoon was prize-giving, and the boys my friends and I had crushes on all won prizes for sports, but Basil kept getting called up to get prizes for Physics and Chemistry and History, Greek and Latin. Tons more. At first everybody clapped but then it got funny. His face got redder and redder every time he went up to get another prize, a book. About a dozen books. Things like Marcus Aurelius."

"Then it was time for tea, before the dance. Everyone milling around or having tea at little tables. Conchi dared me to ask him to dance, so I did. He was standing with his whole family. A big-eared father, mother and three sisters, all with that same unfortunate jaw. I congratulated him, and asked him to dance. And he fell in love, right before my very eyes."

"He had never danced before, so I showed him how easy it was, just making boxes. To 'Siboney.' 'Long Ago and Far Away.' We danced all night, or made boxes. He came to tea every day for a week. Then it was summer vacation and he went to his family's *fundo*. He wrote to me every day, sent me dozens and dozens of poems."

"Tía, how did he kiss?" Mercedes asked.

"Kiss! He never kissed me, didn't even hold my hand. That would have been very serious, in Chile then. I remember feeling faint when Pirulo Diaz held my hand in the movie *Beau Geste*."

"It was a big deal if a boy should address you as *tú*," Sally said. "This was long, long ago. We rubbed alum rocks under our arms for deodorant. Kotex wasn't even invented; we used rags that maids washed over and over."

"And were you in love with Basil, Tía?"

"No. I was in love with Pirulo Diaz. But for years Basil was always there, at our house, at rugby games, at parties. He came to tea every day. Daddy played golf with him, was always asking him to dinner."

"He was the only suitor Daddy ever approved of."

"The worst thing for romance," Mercedes sighed. "Good men are never sexy."

"My Xavier is good! So good to me! And he's sexy," Sally said.

"Basil and Daddy were good in a patronizing and judgemental way. I treated Basil horribly, but he kept coming back. Every single year on my birthday he has sent roses or called me. Year

after year. For over forty years. He has found me through Conchi, or your mother…all kinds of places. Chiapas, New York,
Idaho. Once I was even in a lockup psych ward in Oakland."

"So what has he said, in those phone calls all these years?"

"Very little, actually. About his own life I mean. He is president of a grocery chain. Usually asked how I was. Invariably
something terrible had just happened…our house burned
down or a divorce, a car wreck. Each time he calls he says the
same thing. Like a rosary. Today, on November 12th, he is thinking of the most lovely woman he ever knew. 'Long Ago and Far
Away' plays in the background."

"Year after year!"

"And he never wrote to you or saw you?"

"No," Sally said. "When he called last week to ask where Carlotta was I told him she would be in Mexico City, why not have
lunch with her. I got the feeling he didn't really want to meet
her tomorrow. He said it wouldn't do to tell his wife. I said, why
not bring her along, but he said that wouldn't do."

"Here comes Xavier! You are so lucky, Mamá. You get no
sympathy from us at all. *Pura envidia!*"

Xavier is at her side, holding both her hands. He is married.
Supposedly no one knows about their affair. He has stopped
by, as if by chance. How can everyone not feel the electricity?
Julian smiles at me.

Xavier has changed too, as much as my sister. He is an aristo-
crat, a prominent chemist, used to be very serious and reserved.
Now he laughs too. He and Sally play and they cry and they fight.
They take *danzón* lessons and go to Mérida. They dance the
danzón in the plaza, under the stars, cats and children playing
in the bushes, paper lanterns in the trees.

Everything they say, the most trivial thing like "good morning,
mi vida" or "pass the salt" is charged with such urgency that
Mercedes and I giggle. But we are moved, awed, by these two
people in a state of grace.

Fool to Cry

"Tomorrow is Basil day!" Xavier smiles.

"Victoria and I think she should dress up as a punk, or as an old old lady," Mercedes says.

"Or I could have Sally go in my place!" I say.

"No. Victoria or Mercedes... And he'll think you are still back in the 40s, almost as he remembers you!"

« · »

Xavier and Sally left for her chemo treatment and Mercedes went to work. I spent the day in Coyoacán. In the church the priest was baptizing about fifty babies at once. I knelt at the back, near the bloodiest Christ, and watched the ceremony. The parents and godparents stood in long rows, facing each other in the aisle. The mothers held the babies, dressed in white. Round babies, skinny babies, fat babies, bald babies. The priest walked down the middle of the aisle followed by two altar boys swinging incense censers. The priest prayed in Latin. Wetting his fingers in a chalice he held in his left hand, he made the sign of the cross on each baby's forehead, baptizing them in the name of the Father and the Son and the Holy Ghost. The parents were serious, prayed solemnly. I wished that the priest would bless each mother, too, make some sign, give her some protection.

In Mexican villages, when my sons were infants, Indians would sometimes make the sign of the cross on their brows. *Pobrecito!* they would say. That such a lovely creature should have to suffer this life!

Mark, four years old, in a nursery school on Horatio Street in New York. He was playing pretend house with some other children. He opened a toy refrigerator, poured an imaginary glass of milk and handed it to his friend. The friend smashed the imaginary glass on the floor. Mark's look of pain, the same I have seen later in all my sons during their lives. A wound from

149

an accident, a divorce, a failure. The ferocity of my longing to protect them. My helplessness.

As I leave the church I light a candle beneath the statue of our Blessed Mother Mary. *Pobrecita*.

« · »

Sally is in bed, worn out and nauseated. I put cloths cooled in ice water on her head. I tell her about the people in the plaza at Coyoacán, about the baptism. She tells me about the other patients at chemo, about Pedro, her doctor. She tells me the things Xavier said to her, the tenderness of him, and she cries bitter, bitter tears.

When Sally and I first became friends, after we grew up, we spent several years working out our resentments and jealousies. Later, when both of us were in therapy, we spent years venting our rage at our grandfather, our mother. Our cruel mother. Years later still, our rage at our father, the saint, whose cruelty was not so obvious.

But now we speak only in the present tense. In a *cenote* in the Yucatan, atop Tulum, in the convent in Tepoztlan, in her little room, we laugh with joy at the similarities of our responses, at the stereo of our visions.

« · »

The morning of my 54th birthday we don't stay long at La Vega. Sally wants to rest before her chemo. I need to dress for lunch with Basil. When we get home Mercedes and Victoria are watching a *tele-novela* with Belen and Dolores, the two maids. Belen and Dolores spend most of the day and night watching soap-operas. They have both been with Sally for twenty years; they live in a small apartment on the roof. There is not that much for them to do now that Ramon and the daughters are gone, but Sally would never ask them to leave.

Today is a big day on *Los Golpes de la Vida*. Sally dresses in a robe and comes to watch. I have showered and put on make-up, but stay in my robe too, don't want to wrinkle my grey linen.

Adelina is going to have to tell her daughter Conchita that she can't marry Antonio. Has to confess that Antonio is her natural son, Conchita's brother! Adelina had him in a convent twenty-five years ago.

And there they are in Sanborn's but before Adelina can say a word Conchita tells her mother that she and Antonio have been secretly married. And now they are going to have a baby! Close-up of Adelina's grief-stricken face, her mother's face. But she smiles and kisses Conchita. *Mozo*, she says, do bring us some champagne.

Ok, so it's pretty silly. What was really silly was that all six of us women were bawling our eyes out, just sobbing away when the doorbell rang. Mercedes ran to open the door.

Basil stared at Mercedes, aghast. Not just because she was crying, or wearing shorts and a bra-less top. People are always taken aback by the sisters' beauty. After you are around them awhile you get used to it, like a hare-lip.

Mercedes kissed him on the cheek. "The famous Basil, wearing real English tweeds!"

His face was red. He stared at us, all of us in tears, with such confusion that we got the giggles. Like children do. Serious, punishable giggles. We couldn't stop. I got up, went to give him an *abrazo* too, but again he stiffened, held out his hand for a cool shake.

"Forgive us . . . we're watching a tear-jerker of a *tele-novela*." I introduced him to everyone. "Of course you remember Sally?" He looked aghast again. "My wig!" She ran to put on her wig. I went to dress. Mercedes came with me.

"Come on Tía, dress up real whorish and trashy...he is so stuffy!"

"There is no place to eat around here, surely," Basil was saying.

"Surely, there is. La Pampa, an Argentinian restaurant, just across from the clock of flowers in the park."

"The clock of flowers?"

"I'll show you," I said. "...Let's go."

I followed him down the three flights of stairs, chattering nervously. How good it was to see him, how fit he looked.

In the downstairs foyer he stopped and looked around.

"Ramon is a minister now. Surely he can afford a better place for his family to live?"

"He has a new family now. They live in La Pedregal, a lovely home. But this is a wonderful place, Basil. Sunny and spacious... full of antiques and plants and birds."

"The neighborhood?"

"Calle Amores? Sally would never live any place else. She knows everybody. I even know everybody."

I was greeting people all the way to his car. He had paid some boys to watch it, keep it safe from bandits.

We buckled up.

"What is the matter with Sally's hair?" he asked.

"She lost it because of chemotherapy. She has cancer."

"How terrible! Is the prognosis good?"

"No. She's dying."

"I'm so sorry. I must say, none of you seem particularly affected by it."

"We're all affected by it. Right now we are happy. Sally is in love. She and I have become close, sisters. That's been like falling in love too. Her children are seeing her, hearing her."

He was silent, hands gripping the wheel.

I directed him to the park on Insurgentes.

"Park anywhere, now. See, there is the clock of flowers!"

"It doesn't look like a clock."

"Of course it does. See the numbers! Well, hell, it looked like a clock the other day. The numbers are marigolds, and they've just grown a little leggy. But everybody knows it's a clock."

We parked a long way from the restaurant. It was hot. I have a bad back, smoke a lot. The smog, my high heels. I was faint with hunger. The restaurant smelled wonderful. Garlic and rosemary, red wine, lamb.

"I don't know," he said, "it's very rowdy. It will be hard to have a proper conversation. It's full of Argentines!"

"Well, yeah, it's an Argentine restaurant."

"Your accent is so American! You say 'yeah' all the time."

"Well, yeah, I'm an American."

We walked up and down the street, peering into the windows of one wonderful restaurant after another, but none were quite right, one was too dear. I decided to use the word dear instead of expensive from now on. Oh, look, here's my dear phone bill!

"Basil . . . let's get a *torta* and go sit in the park. I'm famished, and want to spend time talking with you."

"We're going to have to go downtown. Where I am familiar with the restaurants."

"How about I wait here while you go get the car?"

"I don't like to leave you unescorted in this neighborhood."

"This is a swell neighborhood."

"Please. We will go together and find the car."

Find the car. Of course he didn't remember where he had parked the car. Blocks and blocks. We circled back, out, around, ran into the same cats, the same maids leaning on gates flirting with the mailman. The knife sharpener playing a flute, driving his bike with no hands.

I sank back into the cushioned seat of the car, kicking off my shoes. I took out a pack of cigarettes but he asked me not to smoke in the car. Tears were streaking down both of our faces from the Mexico City smog. I said I thought smoking might form a sort of protective screen.

"Ah, Carlotta, still flirting with danger!"

"Let's go. I'm starving."

But he was taking photos of his children from the glove compartment. I held the pictures in their silver frames. Clear-eyed, determined young people. Lantern-jawed. He was talking about their brilliance, their achievements, their successful careers as physicians. Yes, they saw the son, but Marilyn and her mother didn't get on. Both very headstrong.

"She is quite good with servants," Basil said about his wife. "Never lets them step out of bounds. Were those women your sister's servants?"

"They were. They're more like family now."

We turned the wrong way on a one-way street. Basil backed up, cars and trucks honking at us. On the *periférico* then, speeding along, until there was an accident up ahead and we came to a standstill. Basil turned off the motor and the airconditioning. I stepped outside for a smoke.

"You'll get run over!"

Not a car was moving for blocks behind us.

We arrived at the Sheraton at 4:30. The dining room was closed. What to do? He had parked the car. We went into a Denny's next door.

"Denny's is where one ends up," I said.

"I'd like a club sandwich and iced tea," I said. "What are you going to have?"

"I don't know. I find food uninteresting."

I was profoundly depressed. I wanted to eat my sandwich and to go home. But I made polite conversation. Yes, they belonged to an English country club. He played golf and cricket, was in a theatre group. He had played one of the old ladies in *Arsenic and Old Lace*. Great fun.

"By the way. I bought that house, in Chile, with the pool, off the third hole of the golf course in Santiago. We rent it out, but plan to retire there. Do you know which house I mean?"

Fool to Cry

"Of course. A lovely house, with wisteria and lilacs. Look under your lilac bushes, you'll find a hundred golf balls. I always sliced my first shot into that yard."

"What are your plans for retirement? For your future?"

"Future?"

"Do you have savings? IRA, that sort of thing?"

I shook my head.

"I have been very concerned about you. Especially that time when you were in the hospital. You *have* knocked about a bit... three divorces, four children, so many jobs. And your sons, what do they do? Are you proud of them?"

I was irritable, even though my sandwich had arrived. He had ordered an untoasted cheese sandwich and tea.

"I hate that concept... being proud of one's children, taking credit for what they have accomplished. I like my sons. They are loving; they have integrity."

They laugh. They eat a *lot*.

He asked again what they did. A chef, a TV camera man, a graphics designer, a waiter. They all like what they do.

"It doesn't sound as if any of them are in a position to care for you when you'll need it. Oh, Carlotta, if you had only stayed in Chile. You would have had a serene life. You would still be queen of the country club."

"Serene? I would have died in the revolution." Queen of the country club? Change this conversation, quick.

"Do you and Hilda go to the seashore?" I asked.

"How could anyone, after the coast in Chile? No, there are such throngs of Americans. I find the Mexican Pacific boring."

"Basil, how can you possibly find an ocean boring?"

"What do you find boring?"

"Nothing, actually. I've never been bored."

"But then, you have gone to great lengths not to be bored."

Basil moved his almost uneaten sandwich aside and leaned toward me solicitously.

"Dear Carlotta... how ever will you pick up the pieces of your life?"

"I don't want any of those old pieces. I just go along, try not to do any damage."

"Tell me, what do you feel you have accomplished in your life?"

I couldn't think of a thing.

"I haven't had a drink in three years," I said.

"That's scarcely an accomplishment. That's like saying, 'I haven't murdered my mother.'"

"Well, of course, there is that, too." I smiled.

I had eaten all my triangles of sandwiches and the parsley.

"Could I have some flan and a cappuccino, please?"

It was the only restaurant in the Republic of Mexico that didn't have flan. Jello, *sí.*

"What about you, Basil, what of your ambition to be a poet?"

He shook his head. "I still read poetry, of course. Tell me, what line of poetry do you live by?"

What an interesting question! I was pleased, but perversely unacceptable lines came to mind. Say, sea. Take me! Every woman loves a fascist. I love the look of agony / Because I know it's true.

"Do not go gentle into that good night." I didn't even like Dylan Thomas.

"Still my defiant Carlotta! My line is from Yeats: 'Be secret, and exult.'"

God. I stubbed out my cigarette, finished the instant coffee.

"How about 'miles to go before I sleep'? I'd better get back to Sally's."

Traffic and smog were bad. We inched along. He recited all the deaths of people we had known, the financial and marital failures of all my old boyfriends.

He pulled up at the curb. I said goodbye. Foolishly, I moved to give him a hug. He backed away, into the car door. *Ciao*, I said. Exult!

The house was quiet. Sally was asleep, after her chemo. She stirred fitfully. I made some strong coffee, sat by the canaries, near the fragrance of tuberoses, listening to the man downstairs playing his cello badly.

I crept into bed next to my sister. We both slept until it was dark. Victoria and Mercedes came to find out all about the lunch with Basil.

I could have told them about the lunch. I could have made it a very funny story. How the marigolds grew out and Basil couldn't tell it was the clock of flowers. I could have impersonated him acting one of the old ladies in *Arsenic and Old Lace*. But I lay back against the pillow next to Sally.

"He won't ever call me again."

I cried. Sally and her daughters comforted me. They did not think I was a fool to cry.

Mourning

I love houses, all the things they tell me, so that's one reason
I don't mind working as a cleaning woman. It's just like reading
a book.

I've been working for Arlene, at Central Reality. Cleaning
empty houses mostly, but even empty houses have stories, clues.
A love letter stuffed way back in a cupboard, empty whiskey
bottles behind the dryer, grocery lists... "Please pick up Tide, a
package of green linguini and a six pack of Coors. I didn't mean
what I said last night."

Lately I've been cleaning houses where somebody has just
died. Cleaning and helping to sort things for people to take or
to give to Goodwill. Arlene always asks if they have any clothes
or books for the Home for the Jewish Parents, that's where
Sadie, her mother, is. These jobs have been depressing. Either
all the relatives want everything, and argue over the smallest
things, a pair of ratty old suspenders or a coffee mug. Or none
of them want anything to do with anything in the whole house,
so I just pack it all up. In both cases the sad part is how little
time it takes. Think about it. If you should die... I could get rid
of all your belongings in two hours max.

Last week I cleaned the house of a very old black mailman.
Arlene knew him, said he had been bed-ridden with diabetes,
had died of a heart attack. He had been a mean, rigid old guy,
she said, an elder in the church. He was a widower; his wife

had died ten years before. His daughter is a friend of Arlene's, a political activist, on the school board in L.A. "She has done a lot for black education and housing; she's one tough lady," Arlene said, so she must be, since that's what people always say about Arlene. The son is a client of Arlene's, and a different story. A district attorney in Seattle, he owns real estate all over Oakland. "I wouldn't say he is actually a slumlord, but..."

The son and daughter didn't get to the house until late morning, but I already knew a lot about them, from what Arlene told me, and from clues. The house was silent when I let myself in, that echoing silence of a house where nobody's home, where someone just died. The house itself was in a shabby neighborhood in West Oakland. It looked like a small farm house, tidy and pretty, with a porch swing, a well-kept yard with old roses and azaleas. Most of the houses around it had windows boarded up, were sprayed with graffiti. Groups of old winos watched me from sagging porch steps; young crack dealers stood on the corner or sat in cars.

Inside, too, the house seemed far removed from that neighborhood, with lace curtains, polished oak furniture. The old man had spent his time in a big sunroom at the back of the house, in a hospital bed and a wheel chair. There were ferns and African violets crammed on shelves on the windows and four or five bird feeders just outside the glass. A huge new TV and VCR, a compact disc player—presents from his children, I imagined. On the mantel was a wedding picture, he in a tux, his hair slicked back, a pencil-thin moustache. His wife was young and lovely, both were solemn. A photograph of her, old and white-haired, but with a smile, smiling eyes. Solemn the two children's graduation pictures, both handsome, confident, arrogant. The son's wedding picture. A beautiful blonde bride in white satin. A picture of the two of them with a baby girl, about a year old. A picture of the daughter with Congressman Ron

Dellums. On the bed table was a card that began, "Sorry I was just too tied up to make it to Oakland for Christmas..." which could have been from either one of them. The old man's Bible was open to Psalm 104. "The earth shall tremble at the look of him; if he do but touch the hills, they will smoke."

Before they arrived I had cleaned the bedrooms and bathroom upstairs. There wasn't much, but what was in the closets and linen cupboard I stacked in piles on one of the beds. I was cleaning the stairs, turned the vacuum off when they came in. He was friendly, shook my hand; she just nodded and walked up the stairs. They must have come straight from the funeral. He was in a three-piece black suit with a fine gold stripe; she wore a grey cashmere suit, a grey suede jacket. Both of them were tall, strikingly handsome. Her black hair was pulled back into a chignon. She never smiled; he smiled all the time.

I stood behind them as they went through the rooms. He took a carved oval mirror. They didn't want anything else. I asked them if there was anything they could give to the Home for Jewish Parents. She lowered her black eyes at me.

"Do we look Jewish to you?"

He quickly explained to me that people from the Rose of Sharon Baptist Church would be by later to get everything they didn't want. And the Medical Supply place for the bed and wheelchair. He said he'd just pay me now, pulled off four twenties from a big stack of bills held by a silver clip. He said that after I finished cleaning to lock up the house and leave the key with Arlene.

I was cleaning the kitchen while they were in the sun-room. The son took his parents' wedding picture, his own pictures. She wanted their mother's picture. So did he, but he said, No, go ahead. He took the Bible; she took the picture of her and Ron Dellums. She and I helped him carry the TV and VCR and CD player out to the trunk of his Mercedes.

So Long: Stories

"God, it's terrible to look at the neighborhood now," he said. She didn't say anything. I don't think she had looked at it. Back inside she sat in the sunroom and looked around.

"I can't picture Daddy watching birds, or taking care of plants," she said.

"Strange, isn't it? But I don't feel I ever knew him at all."

"He's the one who made us work."

"I remember him whipping you when you got a C in math."

"No," she said, "it was a B. A B plus. Nothing I did was ever good enough for him."

"I know. Still . . . I wish I'd seen him more often. I hate it, how long it was since I came here . . . Yeah, I called him a lot, but . . ."

She interrupted him, telling him not to blame himself, and then they talked about how impossible it would have been for their father to have lived with either of them, how hard it was to get away from their jobs. They tried to make each other feel ok, but you could tell they felt pretty bad.

Me and my big mouth. I wish I would just shut up. What I did was say, "This sunroom is so pleasant. It looks like your father was happy here."

"It does, doesn't it?" the son said, smiling at me, but the daughter glared.

"It's none of your business, whether he was happy or not happy."

"I'm sorry," I said. Sorry I don't slap your mean old mouth.

"I could use a drink," the son said. "There's probably nothing in the house."

I showed him the cupboard where there was brandy and some crème de menthe and sherry. I said how about they move into the kitchen and I could go through the cupboards, show them things before I put them into boxes. They moved to the kitchen table. He poured them both big drinks of brandy. They drank and smoked Kools while I went through the cupboards. Neither of them wanted anything, so it all got packed up quickly.

Mourning

"There are some things in the pantry, though..." I knew because I had my eye on them. An old black cast iron with a carved wooden handle.

"I want that!" they both said.

"Did you mother actually iron with that?" I asked the son.

"No, she used it to make toasted ham and cheese sandwiches. And for corned beef, to press it down."

"I always wondered how people did that..." I said, talking away again, but I shut up because she was looking at me that way.

An old beat-up rolling pin, smoothed from wear, silken.

"I want that!" they both said. She actually laughed then. The drink, the heat in the kitchen had softened her hair-do, wisps curled around her face, shiny now. Her lipstick was gone; she looked like the girl in the graduation picture. He took off his coat and vest and tie, rolled up the sleeves of his shirt. She caught me checking out his fine build and shot me that dagger stare.

Just then the Western Medical Supply came to get the bed and the wheelchair. I took them to the sunroom, opened the back door. When I got back the brother had poured them both another brandy. He leaned toward her.

"Make peace with us," he said. "Come stay for a weekend, get to know Debbie. And you've never seen Latania. She's beautiful, and she looks just like you. Please."

She was silent. But I could see death working on her. Death is healing, it tells us to forgive, it reminds us that we don't want to die alone.

She nodded. "I'll come," she said.

"Oh, that's great!" He put his hand on hers, but she recoiled, her hand moved, grabbed the table like a rigid claw.

Whoa, you are a cold bitch, I said. Not out loud. Out loud I said, "Now here's something you'll both want, I bet." A heavy old cast-iron waffle maker, the kind you put on top of the stove. My grandmother, Mamie, had one. There's nothing like those waffles. Really crisp and brown outside and soft in the center. I put the waffle iron down between them.

She was smiling. "Now this is mine!"

He laughed. "You'll have to pay a fortune in overweight luggage."

"I don't care. Do you remember how Mama would make us waffles when we were sick? With real maple syrup?"

"On Valentine's Day she'd make them in the shape of a heart."

"Only they never looked like hearts."

"No, but we'd say 'Mama, they're exactly like hearts!'"

"With strawberries and whipped cream."

There were other things I brought out then, roasting pans and boxes of canning jars that weren't interesting. The last box, on the top shelf I put on the table.

Aprons. The old-fashioned bib kind. Handmade, embroidered with birds and flowers. Dish towels, embroidered too. All made from flour sacks or gingham from old clothes. Soft and faded, smelling of vanilla and cloves.

"This was made from the dress I wore the first day of fourth grade!"

The sister was unfolding each apron and towel and spreading them all out on the table. Oh. Oh, she kept saying. Tears streaked down her cheeks. She gathered up all the aprons and towels and held them to her breast.

"Mama!" she cried. "Dear, dear Mama!"

The brother was crying now too and he went to her. He embraced her, and she let him hold her, rock her. I slipped out of the room and out the back door.

I was still sitting on the steps when a truck pulled up and three men from the Baptist church got out. I took them around to the front door and upstairs, and told them everything that was to go. I helped one man with the things upstairs, and then helped him load what was in the garage, tools and rakes, a lawnmower and a wheelbarrow.

Mourning

"Well, that's it," one of the men said. The truck backed out and they waved goodbye. I went back inside. The house was silent. The brother and sister had gone. I swept up then and left, locking the doors of the empty house.

Panteón de Dolores

Not "Heavenly Rest" or "Serene Valley." Pantheon of Pain is the name of the cemetery at Chapultepec Park. You can't get away from it in Mexico. Death. Blood. Pain.

Torture is everywhere. In the wrestling matches, Aztec temples, racks of nails in the old convents, bloody thorns on Christs' heads in all the churches. Lord, now all the cookies and candies are made like skulls, since soon it will be the Day of the Dead.

That's the day Mama died, in California. My sister Sally was here, in Mexico City, where she lives. She and her children made an *ofrenda* to our mother.

Ofrendas are fun to make. Offerings to the dead. You make them as pretty as you can. Cascading and brilliant with marigolds and magenta velvets, a flower that looks like brains, and tiny purple sempieternas. The main idea about death here is to make it beautiful and festive. Sultry bleeding Christs, the elegance, the ultimate beautiful deadliness of bullfights, elaborately carved tombs, headstones for the graves.

On the *ofrendas* you place everything the dead person might be wishing for. Tobacco, pictures of his family, mangos, lottery tickets, tequila, postcards from Rome. Swords and candles and coffee. Skulls with friends' names on them. Candy skeletons to eat.

On our mother's *ofrenda* my sister's children had put dozens of Ku Klux Klan figures. She hated them for being the children of a Mexican. Her *ofrenda* had Hershey bars, Jack Daniels, mystery books and many, many dollar bills. Sleeping pills and guns and knives, since she was always killing herself. No noose… she said she couldn't get the hang of it.

I am in Mexico now. This year we made a lovely *ofrenda*, for my sister Sally, who is dying of cancer.

We had masses of flowers, orange, magenta, purple. Many white votive candles. Statues of saints and angels. Tiny guitars and Paris paperweights. Cancun and Portugal. Chile. All the places she had been. Dozens and dozens of skulls with names and pictures of her children, of all of us who have loved her… A picture of Daddy in Idaho, holding her as a baby. Poems from the children who were her students.

« · »

Mama, you weren't in the *ofrenda*. We didn't omit you on purpose. We have, in fact, been saying affectionate things about you these past months.

For years, when Sally and I got together we ranted obsessively about how crazy and cruel you were. But these few months… well, I guess it is natural when one is dying to sort of sum up what has mattered, what has been beautiful. We have remembered your jokes and your way of looking, never missing a thing. You gave us that. Looking.

Not listening though. You'd give us maybe five minutes, to tell you about something, and then you'd say, "Enough."

I can't figure out why our mother hated Mexicans so much. I mean well beyond the given prejudice of all her Texan relatives. Dirty, lying, thieving. She hated smells, any smells, and Mexico smells, even above the exhaust fumes. Onions and carnations. Cilantro, piss, cinnamon, burning rubber, rum and tuberoses. The men smell in Mexico. The whole country smells of sex and soap. That's what terrified you, Mama, you and old

Panteón de Dolores

D. H. Lawrence too. It's easy to get sex and death mixed up here, since they both keep pulsating away. A two-block stroll wafts sensuality, is fraught with peril.

Although today nobody is supposed to go outside at all, because of the pollution level.

My husband and sons and I lived for many years in Mexico. We were very happy during those years. But we always lived in villages, by the sea or in the mountains. There was such an affectionate ease, a passive sweetness there. Or then, as this was many years ago.

Mexico City now... fatalistic, suicidal, corrupt. A pestilential swamp. Oh, but there is a graciousness. There are flashes of such beauty, of kindness and of color you catch your breath.

I went home two weeks ago, for a week, at Thanksgiving, back to the U.S.A. where there is honor and integrity and Lord knows what else, I thought. I got confused. President Bush and Clarence Thomas and anti-abortion and AIDS and Duke and crack and homelessness. And everywhere, MTV, cartoons, ads, magazines—just war and sexism and violence. In Mexico at least a can of cement falls off a scaffold on your head, no Uzis or anything personal.

What I mean is I'm here for an indefinite period. But then what, where will I go?

Mama, you saw ugliness and evil everywhere, in everyone, in each place. Were you crazy or a seer? Either way I can't bear to become like you. I am terrified, I am losing all sense of, what is... precious, true.

Now I'm feeling like you, critical, nasty. What a dump. You hated places with the same passion you hated people... All the mining camps we lived in, the U.S., El Paso, your home, Chile, Peru.

Mullan, Idaho, in the Coeur d'Alene mountains. You hated that mining town the most, because there was actually a little town. "A cliché of a small town." A one-room school, a soda fountain, a post office, a jail. A whore-house, a church. A little lending library at the general store. Zane Grey and Agatha Christie. There was a town hall, with meetings about black-outs and air raids.

You'd rant about the ignorant tacky Finns all the way home. We would stop for a *Saturday Evening Post* and a big Hershey bar before we climbed up the mountain to the mine, with Daddy holding our hands. Dark because the war just started and the windows in the town were blacked out, but the stars and snow were so bright we could see our way perfectly... At home Daddy would read to you until you fell asleep. If it was a really good story you would cry, not because it was sad, just so lovely and everything else in the world was tawdry.

My friend Kentshreve and I would be digging under the lilac bush while you were at the bridge game on Mondays. The three other women would wear housedresses, sometimes even stayed in socks and slippers. It was so cold in Idaho. Often they wore their hair in pin curls and a turban, getting their hair ready for—what? This still is an American custom. You see women everywhere in pink hair rollers. It's some sort of philosophical or fashion statement. Maybe there will be something better, later.

You always dressed carefully. Garter belt. Stockings with seams. A peach satin slip you let show a little on purpose, just so those peasants would know you wore one. A chiffon dress with shoulder pads, a brooch with tiny diamonds. And your coat. I was five years old and even then knew that it was a ratty old coat. Maroon, the pockets stained and frayed, the cuffs stringy. It was a wedding present from your brother Tyler ten years before. It had a fur collar. Oh the poor matted fur, once silver, yellowed now like the peed-on backsides of polar bears in zoos. Kentshreve told me everybody in Mullan laughed at your clothes. "Well, she laughs at all theirs worse, so there."

You'd come teetering up the hill in cheap high heels, your collar turned up around your carefully waved and marcelled bob. A gloved hand grasped the railing of the rickety wooden walk that rose past the mine and the mill. Inside in the living room you'd light the coal stove, kick off your shoes.

You sat in the dark, smoking, sobbing with loneliness and boredom. My mama, Madame Bovary. You read plays. You wished you had been an actress. Noel Coward. *Gas Light*. Anything the Lunts were in, memorizing the lines and saying them out loud while you washed the dishes. "*Oh!* I thought it was your step behind me, Conrad... No. Oh, I *thought* it was your step behind me, Conrad..."

« · »

When Daddy got home, filthy, in heavy miner's boots, a hat with a lamp, he would shower and you'd make cocktails from a little table, with an ice bucket and a seltzer shaker. (This seltzer bottle caused a lot of trouble. Daddy had to remember to buy the cartridges during his rare trips to Spokane. And most visitors resented it. "No, none of that there noisy water. Real water for me.") But that's what they used in plays, and in *The Thin Man* movies.

In *Mildred Pierce* Joan Crawford had a daughter called Sherry, and while the bad guy was spritzing his drink with seltzer he asked Joan Crawford what she wanted to drink.

"I'll take Sherry. Home," she said.

"What a wonderful line!" you said to me as we left the movie theatre. "I think I'll change your name to Sherry, so I can use it."

"How about Cold Beer?" I asked. It was my first witticism. Anyway, it was the first time I made you laugh.

The other time was when Earl the delivery boy had brought a box of groceries from the store. I was helping to put them away. Our house was, in fact, a tar-paper shack, just like you said, and the kitchen floor sloped way to the bottom of the room in undulating waves of rotten linoleum and warped boards. I took out three cans of tomato soup and was going to put them in the cupboard but dropped them. They rolled down the floor and crashed against the wall. I looked up, thought you were going to yell, or hit me, but you were laughing. You took some more cans out of the cupboard and sent them rolling down too.

"Here, let's race!" you said. "My canned corn against your peas!"

We were squatting there, laughing, sailing cans down the room crashing them into the others when Daddy came home.

"Stop that this instant! Put those cans away!" There were lots of cans. (You hoarded them, because of the war, which was a bad thing to do, he said.) It took us a long time to get them all back in the cupboard, both giggling, in whispers, and singing "Praise the loard and paise the ammunition," as you handed cans to me on the floor. It was the best time I ever had with you. We had just got them put away when he came to the door and said, "Go to your room." I went. But he meant for you to go to your room too! It didn't take long after that for me to see that when he sent you to your room it was because you had been drinking.

After that, for as long as I knew you, you were mostly in your room. Deerlodge, Montana, Marion, Kentucky, Patagonia, Arizona, Santiago, Chile. Lima, Peru.

« · »

Sally and I are in her bedroom now in Mexico, have been here most of the time for the last five months. We go out, sometimes, to the hospital for X-rays and lab tests, to have liquid aspirated from her lungs. Twice we have gone out to the Café Paris for coffee, and once to her friend Elizabeth's for breakfast. But she gets very tired. Even her chemo treatments are done in her room now.

We talk and read, I read out loud to her, people come to visit. The sun hits the plants for a little bit in the afternoon. About

Panteón de Dolores

half an hour. She says that in February there is a lot of sun. None of the windows face the sky so the light is not direct, actually, but reflected from the wall next door. In the evening when it gets dark I close the curtains.

Sally and her children have lived here for twenty-five years. Sally isn't like our mother at all, in fact almost annoyingly the opposite, in that she sees beauty and goodness everywhere, in everyone. She loves her room, all the souvenirs on the shelves. We'll sit in the living room and she'll say, "That's my favorite corner, with the fern and the mirror." Or another time she'll say, "That's my favorite corner, with the mask and the basket of oranges."

Me, now, all the corners have me stir crazy.

Sally adores Mexico, with the fervor of a convert. Her husband, her children, her house, everything about her is Mexican. Except her. She's very American, old-fashioned American, wholesome. In a way I am the more Mexican, my nature is dark. I have known death, violence. Most days I don't even notice that period when the room has sunlight in it.

《 · 》

When our father went to war Sally was just a baby. We went by train from Idaho to Texas to live with our grandparents for the Duration. Duro = Hard.

One thing that made Mama the way she was was that when she was little their life was very easy and gracious. Her mother and father were from the best Texan families. Grandpa was a wealthy dentist; they had a beautiful home with servants, a nanny for Mama, who spoiled her, as did three older brothers. Then wham bam she got run over by a Western Union boy and was in the hospital almost a year. During that year everything got worse. The Depression, Grandpa's gambling, his drinking. She got out of the hospital to find her world changed. A shabby house down by the smelter, no car, no servants, no room of her own. Her mother, Mamie, working as Grandpa's nurse, no longer playing mah-jongg and bridge. Everything was grim. And scary probably, if Grandpa did to her what he did to both Sally and me. She never said anything about it, but he must have, since she hated him so much, would never let anybody touch her, not even shake hands...

The train neared El Paso as the sun came up. It was awesome to see, the space, the wide open spaces, coming from the dense pine forests. As if the world were uncovered, a lid taken off. Miles and miles of brightness and blue, blue sky. I ran back and forth from windows on each side of the club car that had finally opened, thrilled by this whole new face of the earth.

"It's just the desert," she said. "Deserted. Empty. Arid. And pretty soon we'll be pulling into the hell-hole I used to call home."

Sally wanted me to help her get her house on Calle Amores in order. Sort photographs, clothes and papers, fix shower curtain rods, window panes. Except for the front door, none of the doors had doorknobs; you had to use a screwdriver to get in the closets and prop the bathroom door shut with a basket. I called some workmen to come and put in doorknobs. They came and that was ok except they came on a Sunday afternoon while we were having a family dinner and they stayed until about ten at night. What happened was that they put on the doorknobs but didn't tighten any screws, so each doorknob that any of us tried fell off in our hands and then you couldn't open the closet doors at all. Also many screws rolled off and disappeared. I called the men the next day and a few days later they came in the morning, just when my sister had fallen asleep after a bad night. The three of them made so much noise I said forget it, my sister is sick, grave, and you're too loud. Come back another time. I went back into her room but later began to hear some huffing and panting and muffled thuds. They were taking all the doors off the hinges so they could carry them up to the roof to fix them without making any noise.

Am I really just mad because Sally's dying, so get mad at a whole country? The toilet is broken now. They need to take out the entire floor.

I miss the moon. I miss solitude.

In Mexico there is never not anyone else there. If you go in your room to read somebody will notice you're by yourself and go keep you company. Sally is never alone. At night I stay until I am sure she is asleep.

There is no guide to death. No one to tell you what to do, how it's going to be.

When we were little our grandmother, Mamie, took over Sally's care. At night Mama ate and drank and read mysteries in her room. Grandpa ate and drank and listened to the radio in his room. Actually Mama was gone most nights, with Alice Pomeroy and the Parker girls, playing bridge or in Juarez. During the day she went to Beaumont hospital to be a Gray Lady, where she read to blind soldiers and played bridge with maimed ones.

She was fascinated by anything grotesque, just like Grandpa was, and when she got back from the hospital she would call Alice and tell her about all the soldiers' wounds, their war stories, how their wives left when they found out they had no hands or feet.

Sometimes she and Alice went to a U.S.O. dance, looking for a husband for Alice. Alice never found a husband, worked at the Popular Dry Goods as a seam ripper until she died.

Byron Merkel worked at the Popular too, in lamps. He was supervisor of lamps. He was still madly in love with Mama after all these years. They had been in the Thespian Club in high school and starred in all the plays. Mama was very small, but still in all the love scenes they had to sit down because he was only five feet two. Otherwise he would have gone on to be a famous actor.

He took her to plays. *Cradle Song. The Glass Menagerie.* Sometimes he'd come over in the evenings and they'd sit on the porch swing. They'd read plays they performed in when they were young. I was always under the porch then in a little nest I had made with an old blanket and a cookie tin with saltines in it. *The Importance of Being Earnest. The Barretts of Wimpole Street.*

He was a teetotaller. I thought that meant he only drank tea, which was all he drank, while she drank Manhattans. That's what they were doing when I heard him tell her he was still madly in love with her after all these years. He said he knew he couldn't hold a candle to Ted (Daddy), another strange expression. He was always saying, "Well, it's a long road to Ho," which I couldn't make out either. Once, when Mama was complaining about Mexicans he said, "Well, give them an inch and they'll take an inch." The trouble with the things he said was he had a deep projecting tenor voice, so every word seemed weighted with significance, echoed in my mind. Teetotaller, teetotaller…

One night after he had gone home she came in, to the bedroom where I slept with her. She kept on drinking and crying and scribbling, literally scribbling, in her diary.

"Are you okay?" I finally asked her, and she slapped me.

"I told you to stop saying 'okay'!" Then she said she was sorry she got mad at me.

"It's that I hate living on Upson Street. All your Daddy ever writes me about is his ship, and not to call it a boat. And the only romance in my life is a midget lamp salesman!"

This sounds funny now, but it wasn't then when she was sobbing, sobbing, as if her heart would break. I patted her and she flinched. She hated to be touched. So I just watched her by the light of the street lamp through the window screen. Just watched her weep. She was totally alone, like my sister Sally is when she weeps that way.

Dust to Dust

Michael Templeton was a hero, an Adonis, a star. Truly a hero, a much decorated bombardier in the RAF. When he returned to Chile after the war he had been a star rugby and cricket player for the Prince of Wales team. He raced his BSA for the British motorcycle team and had been the champion for three years. Never lost a race. He even won the last one before he spun out and hit the wall.

He had arranged for Johnny and me to have seats in the press box. Johnny was Michael's little brother and my best friend. He idolized Michael as much as I did. Johnny and I felt disdain for everything then and a contempt for most people, especially our teachers and parents. We even conceded, with some scorn, that Michael was a cad. But he had style, cachet. All the girls and women, even old women, were in love with him. A slow, slow low voice. He gave Johnny and me rides on the beach in Algarrobo. Flying over hard wet sand, scattering flocks of gulls, their wing beats louder than the motor, than the ocean. Johnny never made fun of me for being in love with Michael, gave me snapshots and clippings in addition to the ones we helped his Mum paste in scrapbooks.

His parents didn't go to the race. They were at the dining room table having tea and bikkies. Mr. Templeton's tea was rum, really, in the blue cup. Michael's mum was crying, sick with worry about the race. He'll be the death of me, she said.

Mr. Templeton said he hoped Mike would break his bloody fool neck. It wasn't just the race...this was pretty much their daily conversation. Even though he was a hero, Michael still had no job after three years back from the war. He drank and gambled and got into serious troubles with women. Whispered phone calls and late night visits from fathers or husbands, slamming doors. But women just became even more fascinated with him and people actually insisted upon loaning him money.

The stadium was crowded and festive. The racers and pit crews were glamorous, dashing Italians, Germans, Australians. The main contenders were the British team and the Argentines. The English rode BSAs and Nortons; the Argentines Motoguzzis. None of the racers had Michael's panache, his nonchalance or white scarf. What I am saying is that even with the shock of his death, even with the bike in flames, with Michael's blood on the concrete wall, his body, the shrieking and the sirens, it all had his particular throwaway insouciance. That it was the last race, and he had won it. Johnny and I didn't speak, not about the terror, nor about the drama of it.

The dining room at home was buzzing and crowded. Mrs. Templeton had frizzed her hair and powdered her face. She was saying that it would be the death of her but in fact she was very lively, making tea and passing scones and answering the telephone. Mr. Templeton kept on saying "I told him he would break his bloody neck! I told him!" Johnny reminded him that he had said he wished Michael would.

It was exciting. Nobody but me had visited the Templetons for years, and now the house was full. There were reporters from the *Mercurio* and the *Pacific Mail*. Our "Michael album" was open on the table. People were saying hero and prince and tragic waste all over the house. Groups of beautiful girls were upstairs and downstairs. One of the girls would be sobbing while two or three others patted her and brought her tissues.

Dust to Dust

Johnny and I kept up our usual stance of mirthful scorn. We had not actually realized that Michael was dead, didn't until the Saturday night after the funeral. That was when we used to sit on the rim of the tub while he shaved, humming "Saturday night is the loneliest night in the week." He'd tell us all about his "birds," listing their attributes and inevitable, very funny, flaws. The Saturday after he died we just sat in the tub. We didn't cry, just sat in the tub, talking about him.

We had fun, though, watching the flurry before the funeral, the rivalries between the mourning girlfriends. Most amazing of all was the way the entire British colony of Santiago decided that Michael had died for the King. Glory to the Empire, the *Pacific Mail* said. Mrs. Templeton was peppy, had us and the maids beating rugs and oiling bannisters and baking more scones. Mr. Templeton just sat with his blue cup muttering how Mike never could take direction, had been hell-bent.

I was allowed to leave school for the burial. I wouldn't have gone at all but there was a chemistry test second period. After that I took off my school apron and went to my locker. I was very solemn and brave.

There are things people just don't talk about. I don't mean the hard things, like love, but the awkward ones, like how funerals are fun sometimes or how it's exciting to watch buildings burning. Michael's funeral was wonderful.

In those days there were still horse-drawn hearses. Massive creaking wagons drawn by four or six black horses. The horses wore blinders and were covered in thick black net, with tassles that dragged dusty in the streets. The drivers wore tails and top hats and carried whips. Because of Michael's hero status many organizations had contributed to the funeral, so that there were six hearses. One was for his body, the others for flowers. Mourners followed the hearses to the cemetery in black cars.

During the service at Saint Andrew's (high) Anglican church many of the sad girls fainted or had to be led away because they

were so overcome. Outside the gaunt and jaunty drivers smoked
on the curb in their top hats. Some people always associate the
heady smell of flowers with funerals. For me it needs to be mixed
with the scent of horse manure. Parked outside too were over
a hundred motorcycles which would follow the cortege to the
cemetery. Gunnings of engines, splutters, smoke, backfires. The
drivers in black leather, with black helmets, their team colors
on their sleeves. It would have been in poor taste for me to tell
the girls at school just how many unbelievably handsome men
had been at that funeral. I did anyway.

I rode in the car with the Templetons. All the way to the
cemetery Mr. Templeton fought with Johnny about Michael's
helmet. Johnny held it on his lap, planned to place it in the grave
with Michael. Mr. Templeton argued, reasonably, that helmets
were hard to come by and very dear. You had to get someone
to bring them from England or America, and pay a stiff duty
for them too. "Sell it to some other sod to race in," he insisted.
Johnny and I exchanged glances. Wouldn't you know he'd only
care about the cost?

More glances and grins between us in the cemetery itself with
all the tombs and crypts and angels. We decided to be buried at
sea and promised to attend to that, for each other.

The Canon, in white lace over a purple cassock, stood at the
head of the grave, surrounded by the British racing team, their
helmets crooked in their arms. Noble and solemn, like knights.
As Michael's body was lowered into the ground the Canon said,
"Man, that is born of woman, hath but a short time to live, and
is full of misery. He cometh up, and is cut down, like a flower."
While he was saying that Odette tossed in a red rose and then
so did Conchi and then Raquel. Defiantly, Millie stalked up and
threw in a whole bouquet.

It was lovely then what the Canon said over the grave. He said,
"Thou shalt show me the path of life. In Thy presence is the
fullness of joy, and at Thy right hand there is pleasure for ever

more." Johnny smiled. I could tell he thought that was just what to say for Michael. Johnny looked around, to be sure it was the end of the roses, stepped to the rim of the grave and tossed in Michael's helmet. Ian Frazier, closest to the grave, cried out with grief and impulsively threw his own helmet on top of Michael's. Pop pop pop then, as if mesmerized, each member of the British racing team tossed his helmet upon the casket. Not just filling the grave but mounding it up with black domes like a pile of olives. Most merciful Father, the Canon was saying as the two grave diggers piled earth upon the mound and covered it with wreaths of flowers. The mourners sang *God Save the King*. Upon the faces of the race drivers were expressions of sorrow and loss. Everyone filed sadly away and then there was a clatter and roar of motorcycles and an echoing and clatter of hooves as the hearses galloped off, careening dangerously, whips cracking, the tails of the drivers' black coats flapping in the wind.

So Long

I love to hear Max say hello.

I called him when we were new lovers, adulterers. The phone rang, his secretary answered and I asked for him. Oh, hello, he said. Max? I was faint, dizzy, in the phone booth.

We've been divorced for many years. He is an invalid now, on oxygen, in a wheelchair. When I was living in Oakland he used to call me five or six times a day. He has insomnia: once he called at three a.m. and asked if it was morning yet. Sometimes I'd get annoyed and hang up right away or else I wouldn't answer the phone.

Most of the time we talked about our children, our grandson or Max's cat. I'd file my nails, sew, watch the A's game while we talked. He's funny, and a good gossip.

I have lived in Mexico City for almost a year now. My sister Sally is very ill. I take care of her house and children, bring her food, give her injections, baths. I read to her, wonderful books. We talk for hours, cry and laugh, get mad at the news, worry about her son out late.

It is uncanny, how close we have become. We have been together all day for so long. We see and hear things the same way, know what the other is going to say...

I rarely leave the apartment. None of the windows look out onto the sky, just onto airshafts or the apartments next door.

So Long: Stories

You can see the sky from Sally's bed, but I only see it when I open and close her curtains. I speak Spanish with her and her children, everybody.

Actually Sally and I don't talk that much anymore. It hurts her lung to talk. I read, or sing, or we just lie together in the dark, breathing in unison.

I feel I have vanished. Last week in the Sonora market I was so tall, surrounded by dark Indians, many of them speaking in Nahuatl. Not only was I vanished I was invisible. I mean for a long time I believed I wasn't there at all.

Of course I have a self here, and a new family, new cats, new jokes. But I keep trying to remember who I was in English.

《 · 》

That's why I'm so glad to hear from Max. He calls a lot, from California. Hello, he says. He tells me about hearing Percy Heath, about protesting the death penalty at San Quentin. Our son Keith made him eggs benedict on Easter Sunday. Nathan's wife, Linda, told Max not to phone her so much. Our grandson Nikko said he was falling asleep in spite of himself.

Max tells me the traffic and weather reports, describes the clothes on the Elsa Clench show. He asks me about Sally.

In Albuquerque, when we were young, before I met him, I had listened to him play saxophone, watched him race Porsches at Fort Sumpter. Everybody knew who he was. He was handsome, rich, exotic. Once I saw him at the airport, saying goodbye to his father. He kissed his father goodbye, with tears in his eyes. I want a man who kisses his father goodbye I thought.

When you are dying it is natural to look back on your life, to weigh things, to have regrets. I have done this, too, along with my sister these last months. It took a long time for us both to let go of anger and blame. Even our regret and self-recrimination lists get shorter. The lists now are of what we're

184

So Long

left with. Friends. Places. She wishes she were dancing *danzón* with her lover. She wants to see the *parroquia* in Veracruz, palm trees, lanterns in the moonlight, dogs and cats among the dancers' polished shoes. We remember one-room school houses in Arizona, the sky when we skied in the Andes.

She has stopped worrying about her children, what will become of them when she dies. I will probably resume worrying about mine after I leave here, but now we simply drift slowly through the patterns and rhythms of each new day. Some days are full of pain and vomit, others are calm, with a marimba playing far away, the whistle of the *camote* man at night...

I don't regret my alcoholism any more. Before I left California my youngest son, Joel, came to breakfast. The same son I used to steal from, who had told me I wasn't his mother. I cooked cheese blintzes; we drank coffee and read the paper, muttering to each other about Rickie Henderson, George Bush. Then he went to work. He kissed me and said So long, Ma. So long, I said.

All over the world mothers are having breakfast with their sons, seeing them off at the door. Can they know the gratitude I felt, standing there, waving? The reprieve.

I was nineteen when my first husband left me. I married Jude then, a thoughtful man with a dry sense of humor. He was a good person. He wanted to help me bring up my two baby sons.

Max was our best man. After the wedding, in the back yard, Jude went off to work, where he played piano at Al Monte's bar. My best friend Shirley, the other witness, left almost without speaking. She was very upset about me marrying Jude, thinking I had done it out of desperation.

Max stayed. After the children went to bed we sat around eating wedding cake and drinking champagne. He talked about Spain; I talked about Chile. He told me about the years in Harvard with Jude and Creeley. About playing saxophone when bebop began. Charlie Parker and Bud Powell, Dizzy Gillespie. Max had been a heroin addict during those bebop days. I didn't know what that meant then, actually. Heroin to me had a nice connotation... Jane Eyre, Becky Sharp, Tess.

Jude played at night. He woke late in the afternoon, then he would practice or he and Max would play duets for hours and then we'd have supper. He went off to work. Max would help me do the dishes and put the children to bed.

I couldn't bother Jude at work. When there was a prowler, when the kids got sick, when I got a flat tire it was Max I called. Hello, he said.

Well, anyway, after a year we had an affair. It was intense and passionate, a big mess. Jude wouldn't talk about it. I left him to live by myself with the children. Jude showed up and told me to get into the car. We were going to New York, where Jude would play jazz and we would save our marriage.

We never did discuss Max. We both worked hard in New York. Jude practiced and jammed, played Bronx weddings, strip shows in Jersey until he got into the union. I made children's clothes that even sold at Bloomingdales. We were happy. New York was wonderful then. Allen Ginsberg and Ed Dorn read at the Y. The Mark Rothko show at MOMA, during the big snowstorm. The light was intense from the snow through the skylights; the paintings pulsated. We heard Bill Evans and Scott La Faro. John Coltrane on soprano sax. Ornette's first night at the Five Spot.

In the daytime, while Jude slept, the boys and I took the subway all over the city, getting off each day at new stops. We rode ferries, over and over. Once, when Jude was playing at Grossinger's, we camped out in Central Park. That's how nice New York was then, or how dumb I was...We lived on Greenwich Street down by the Washington Market, by Fulton Street.

Jude made a red toy box for the boys, hung swings from the pipes in our loft. He was patient and stern with them. At night when he got home we made love. All the anger and sadness and tenderness between us electric in our bodies. It was never spoken out loud.

So Long

At night when Jude was at work I read to Ben and Keith, sang them to sleep and then I sewed. I called the Symphony Sid program and asked him to play Charlie Parker and King Pleasure until he told me not to call so often. Summers were very hot and we slept on the roof. Winters were cold and there was no heat after five or on weekends. The boys wore ear-muffs and mittens to bed. Steam came out of my mouth as I sang to them.

In Mexico now I sing King Pleasure songs to Sally. "Little Red Top." "Parker's Blues." "Sometimes I'm Happy."

It's pretty horrible when there is nothing else you can do.

In New York when the phone rang at night it was Max.

Hello, he said.

He was racing in Hawaii. He was racing in Wisconsin. He was watching TV, thinking of me. Iris were blooming in New Mexico. Flash floods in arroyos in August. Cottonwoods turned yellow in the fall.

He came to New York often, to hear music, but I never saw him. He would call and tell me all about New York and I would tell him all about New York. Marry me, he said, give me a reason to live. Talk to me, I said, don't hang up.

« · »

One night it was bitterly cold, Ben and Keith were sleeping with me, in snowsuits. The shutters banged in the wind, shutters as old as Herman Melville. It was Sunday so there were no cars. Below in the streets the sailmaker passed, in a horse-drawn cart. Clop clop. Sleet hissed cold against the windows and Max called. Hello, he said. I'm right around the corner in a phone booth.

He came with roses, a bottle of brandy and four tickets to Acapulco. I woke up the boys and we left.

It's not true, what I said about no regrets, although I felt not the slightest regret at the time. This was just one of the many things I did wrong in my life, leaving like that.

So Long: Stories

The Plaza Hotel was warm. Hot, in fact. Ben and Keith got into the steaming bath with an expression of awe, as if into a Texan baptism. They fell asleep on clean white sheets. In the adjoining room Max and I made love and we talked until morning.

We drank champagne over Illinois. We kissed while the boys slept across from us and clouds billowed outside the window. When we landed, the sky above Acapulco was streaked coral and pink.

The four of us swam and then ate lobster and swam some more. In the morning the sun shone through the wooden shutters making stripes on Max and Ben and Keith. I sat up in bed, looking at them, with happiness.

Max would carry each boy to bed and tuck him in. Kiss him sweet, the way he had kissed his father. Max slept as deeply as they. I thought he must be exhausted from what we were doing, his leaving his wife, taking on a family.

He taught them both to swim and to snorkel. He told them things. He told me things. Just things, about life, people he knew. We interrupted each other telling him things back. We lay on the fine sand on Caleta beach, warm in the sun. Keith and Ben buried me in the sand. Max's finger tracing my lips. Bursts of color from the sun against my closed sandy eyelids. Desire.

In the evenings we went to a park by the docks where they rented tricycles. Max and I held hands as the boys raced furiously around the park, flashing past pink bougainvillaea, red canna lilies. Beyond them ships were being loaded on the docks.

One afternoon my mother and father, chatting away, walked up the gangplank to the S.S. Slavengerfjord, a Norwegian ship. My sister had written to me that they were traveling from Tacoma to Valparaiso. My parents weren't speaking to me then, because of my marriage to Jude. I couldn't call out to them and say, Hi Mama! Hi Daddy! Isn't this a coincidence? This is Max.

So Long

But it made me feel good, to know my parents were right there. And now they were at the railings as the ship sailed out to sea. My father was sunburnt and wore a floppy white hat. My mother smoked. Ben and Keith just kept riding faster and faster around the cement track, calling to one another, and to us...Look at me!

Today there was a big gas explosion in Guadalajara, hundreds of people killed, their homes destroyed. Max called to see if I was all right. I told him how everybody in Mexico thinks it's funny now to go around asking, "Say...do you smell gas?"

In Acapulco we made friends at the hotel. Don and Maria, who had a six-year-old daughter, Lourdes. In the evenings the children would color on their terrace until they fell asleep.

We stayed very late, until the moon grew high and pale. Don and Max played chess by the light of a kerosene lantern. Caress of moths. Maria and I lay crosswise on a big hammock, talking softly about silly things like clothes, about our children, love. She and Don had been married only six months. Before she met him she had been very alone. I told her how in the morning I said Max's name before I even opened my eyes. She said her life had been like a dreary record over and over each day and now in a second the record was turned over, music. Max overheard her and he smiled at me. See, *amor*, we're the flip side now.

We had some other friends, too. Raúl, the diver and his wife Soledad. One weekend the six of us steamed clams on the terrace of our hotel. All the children had been sent to take naps. But one by one different children would pop up, wanting to watch what was going on. Back to bed! Another would want water, another just plain couldn't sleep. Back to bed. Keith came out and said he saw a giraffe! Now go back to bed, we'll wake you soon. Ben came out and said there were tigers and elephants. Oh for God's sake. But there it was in the street beneath us. A circus parade. We woke all the children then. One of the circus men thought Max was a movie star so they gave us free tickets.

So Long: Stories

We all went to the circus that night. It was magical, but the children fell asleep before the end of the trapeze act.

There was an earthquake in California today. Max called to say that it wasn't his fault and he can't find his cat.

It was the ghostly setting moon that shone upon us as we made love that night. We lay next to each other then under the wooden revolving fan, hot, sticky. Max's hand on my wet hair. Thank you, I whispered, to God, I think...

In the mornings when I woke his arms would be around me, his lips against my neck, his hand on my thigh.

One day I woke before the sun came up and he wasn't there. The room was silent. He must be swimming, I thought. I went into the bathroom. Max was sitting on the toilet, cooking something in a blackened spoon. A syringe was on the sink.

"Hello," he said.

"Max, what is that?"

"It's heroin," he said.

《 · 》

That sounds like the end of a story, or the beginning, when really it was just a part of the years that were to come. Times of intense technicolor happiness and times that were sordid and frightening.

We had two more sons, Nathan and Joel. We traveled all over Mexico and the United States in a Beechcraft Bonanza. We lived in Oaxaca, finally settled in a village on the coast of Mexico. We were happy, all of us, for a long time and then it became hard and lonely because he loved heroin much more.

Not detox...Max says on the phone...Retox, that's what everybody needs. And Just say no? You should say No, thank you. He is joking, he hasn't been on drugs for many years now.

For months Sally and I worked hard trying to analyze our

So Long

lives, our marriages, our children. She never even drank or smoked like I did.

Her ex-husband is a politician. He stops by almost every day, in a car with two bodyguards, and two escort cars with men in them. Sally is as close to him as I am with Max. So what is marriage anyway? I never figured it out. And now it is death I don't understand.

Not just Sally's death. My country, after Rodney King and the riots. All over the world, the rage and despair.

Sally and I write rebuses to each other so she doesn't hurt her lung talking. Rebus is where you draw pictures instead of words or letters. Violence, for example, is a viola and some ants. Sucks is somebody drinking through a straw. We laugh, quietly, in her room, drawing. Actually, love is not a mystery for me anymore. Max calls and says hello. I tell him that my sister will be dead soon. How are you? he asks.